THE LIFE AND TIME OF LONNY QUICKE

THE LIFE AND TIME OF LONNY QUICKE

Kirsty Applebaum

nosy
crow

First published in the UK in 2021 by Nosy Crow Ltd
The Crow's Nest, 14 Baden Place
Crosby Row, London SE1 1YW

www.nosycrow.com

ISBN: 978 1 78800 524 1

Nosy Crow and associated logos are trademarks and/or registered
trademarks of Nosy Crow Ltd

Text copyright © Kirsty Applebaum, 2021
Cover and inside illustration copyright © Matt Saunders, 2021
Title lettering © David Dean, 2021

The right of Kirsty Applebaum to be identified as the author of this
work has been asserted.

A CIP catalogue record for this book is available from the
British Library.

Printed and bound in the UK by Clays Ltd, Elcograf S.p.A.
Typeset by Tiger Media

Papers used by Nosy Crow are made from wood grown in
sustainable forests

1 3 5 7 9 10 8 6 4 2

For my mum and dad

Part 1: FARSTOKE

CHAPTER 1

Vvvvvmmmmm
   The buzzing.
   In the roots of my teeth.
   Vvvvvmmmmmmmmmmmm
   In the thick of my tongue.
   I search around on the shady forest floor.
   Nothing.
   I pull apart flat, feathered fern leaves.
   Nothing.
   Vvvvvvvvvvvvmmmmmmmmmmmmmmm
   I push bracken aside with my size tens. *Clodhoppers*, Grandad calls them.
   Nothing.

Where is it? I let the bracken bounce back.

Must be here somewhere. The buzzing's never wrong.

"Lonny – wait for me!" Midge stumbles through the trees, that ridiculous yellow baseball cap stuck backwards on his head. "What're you doing?" he says. "What happened?"

I look down. The basket's on its side, ink caps scattered over the ground. Must've dropped it.

Midge rights the basket and scoops the mushrooms back in. His sleeves are too long for his arms. He has to stop to roll them up.

Vvvvvvvvvvvvvvmmmmmmmmmmmmmmmmm

My jaw vibrates.

"Lonny?" Midge frowns. "You've got the buzzing again, haven't you?"

Vvvvvvvvvvvvvvmmmmmmmmmmmmmmmmm

"We should go back home," he says. "Dad said you have to walk away if you get the buzzing."

Walk away.

"C'mon." He yanks at my sleeve, but he's tiny, Midge is. No match for big brother Lonny. I push him off, hold him behind me with one arm, and keep on looking.

Ah.

There.

A rabbit. Breathing tight little dying-rabbit breaths. Twitching.

It's not got long. Must've been got by a fox, unlucky

beggar.

Or a stoat.

I kneel down – at the head end, mind. The rest's all blood-stuck and askew. I reach out a finger. Stroke its ear.

Feels soft. And warm. Like kisses and kind words from your mother. And I haven't had either of those in a very long time, so I keep on stroking.

"Lonny! Don't, Lonny!" Midge, all fretty. "Leave it alone. Walk away. It's just a rabbit. We shouldn't even have come out this far. Should've stopped at the oaks. Let's go home." Tug, tug, tug at my sleeve.

I shake him off.

Vvvvvvvvvvvvvvvmmmmmmmmmmmmmmmmmm

The buzzing shifts. Shudders down my neck. Squeezes past my shoulder, my elbow, my hand. Pushes out through the ends of my fingers.

The rabbit stops twitching.

Its breathing slows.

Dead?

No.

Wait.

The breathing doesn't stop; it just slows to regular. Then the little rabbit legs twist themselves round and the dark rabbit blood dries itself up and everything slides nice 'n' smooth back into place. Like magic.

It gets up, gives itself a shake, and hops off.

And the buzzing's gone.

"You shouldn't have done that," says Midge.

"What's Dad going to say?"

"Who's going to tell him?"

He looks at the ground where the rabbit was.

I sit back on my heels.

Calm teeth.

Calm tongue.

Calm head.

OK, so I've aged again. Voice got a little bit deeper, arms grown a little bit longer. But it was only a rabbit. It'll shorten a few days from me, a week at the most. Talents like this don't come free, you know. There's always a price.

Give a bit of life, lose a bit of life.

That's how it goes.

Breathe, Lonny.

Breathe.

"Lonny?"

"Mmmm?"

Breathe.

"Did you hear that?" Midge. Fretting again.

"Mmmm?"

Breathe.

"Did you hear it?"

"Did I hear what?"

Yap!

"That," he says.

I open my eyes.

Yap-yap!

Yap! Yap!

A dog darts out from the trees.

What. On. Earth?

A dog, in the middle of the forest?

In the middle of *our* forest?

Yap!

It runs towards us.

Midge's hands clench up. "Told you we shouldn't have come out this far."

It's a little white quiver of a thing, with a luminous pink collar, twigs for legs and a whipped-under tail. Not much use for anything at all, I shouldn't imagine. Except trouble.

Yap! Yap-Yap!

It jumps up at Midge and – guess what – he falls over.

Unbelievable.

The dog slurps at his face.

"Lonny! Get it off me! Get it off!"

"Shush, Midge. Keep quiet."

Thing about dogs is, they don't wander around forests by themselves. Especially quivery little dogs like this. There'll be people following after, sooner or later.

I listen.

"*Suuuuuu-keeeeeey!*"

There you go.

Suki. That's her name, then.

The dog – *Suki* – stops still, two front feet on Midge's chest. She cocks an ear.

"*Suuuuuu-keeeeeey! Where are you?*"

"Get it off me, Lonny!"

"Keep quiet. We got to get ourselves away from this dog." I grab the skinny thing round her middle.

Grrrrrrrrr.

She twists round and looks me all beady in the eye.

Grrrrrrrrrrrrrrrrrrrrrr.

The growl comes from deep in her belly. I feel it through my fingers.

Midge scrambles to his feet, I stick Suki on the ground, and we run.

Crackle! Crunch! Snap! I dodge between ash and birch and hazel. The ground crumbles under my boots.

"Lonny! Wait for me!"

I stop for Midge to catch up. Suki gallops past him and skids to a halt in front of me.

She bares her teeth. *Grrrrrrrrrrrrr.*

"Go!" I tell her. "Go on. Go away!"

Grrrrrrrrrrrrrrrrrrrrrr.

It's a big sound for a tiny dog. Her legs tremble.

"Suuuuuuuu-keeeey! Suuuuuuuu-keeeeeey!"

"Lonny, they're gonna find us." Midge looks at the forest behind him. He swishes a mayfly out of his face.

Grrrrrrrrrrrrr.

"Suki – is that you?" Voices getting closer. "Erin! Over here. I can hear her. This way! You're a bad dog, Suki!" A flash of orange anorak between the trees.

"Lonny!" Midge swishes at another mayfly. "What

are we gonna do?"

Mayflies.

The air's full of them.

"Lonny!"

We must be near the stream. "C'mon." I grab Midge's arm and pull him through the trees.

There it is.

Cool and fresh and buzzing with life.

"Quick." I wade in. *Slooooooosh.*

Midge stares at the water. "I can't go in there."

Oh, for heaven's sake. "It's hardly even going to be up to your knees." I yank him in after me.

It's not that deep but it's cold as anything and flowing fast, so it's enough to put the little dog off. We scramble out the other side, hide behind a yew tree and shiver.

Grrrrrrrrrrrr. Suki growls on the far bank.

"Suki! You're a bad dog. A really bad dog!" It's a girl, not much bigger than Midge. "You mustn't keep running off like this. I found her, Erin. I found her!" She gathers up the trembly dog and kisses her all over. Clips a luminous pink lead on to the luminous pink collar. Suki licks her face. *Yap! Yap-Yap!*

Another girl comes out from the trees – older than the first. She strokes Suki's head. Suki licks at her hand. Seems Suki likes pretty much everyone, except for me.

"Well done, Katy," she says.

Katy.

Erin and Katy.

"And well done, Suki, *not*. You've got us proper lost now. How are we going to get back home? Dad'll be livid." She pulls something out of her pocket and peers at it. A mobile phone. I've seen them on Dad's TV.

"Course," she says, "it'd help if we lived somewhere you could actually get a signal. Like *anywhere else in the universe.*"

"Um…" Katy turns round on the spot, clutching Suki to her chest. She stops and points. "I think it's this way."

"All right, then," says Erin. "That way it is. You'd better be right."

"I am right – I'm sure I am. Farstoke, here we come." They march off eastwards.

I lean back against the yew tree. Safe.

"Farstoke," whispers Midge. "Did you hear that, Lonny? They're from Farstoke."

I heard it.

Midge sits on the ground. "Told you we'd come too far." He swishes another couple of mayflies away.

I look up. There's a whole cloud of them under the branches. Hundreds. Thousands. So many the air over our heads isn't even properly see-through any more. They dance and dive and swoop and zoom. Having the time of their lives.

Those girls are gonna be a long while getting back to Farstoke. Should be heading southwards, not eastwards.

"Lonny?" Midge sniffs.

"Mmmm?"

"Can we go home now?"

We wade back through the stream, squeeze the water out from the bottom of our trousers, and set off for home.

CHAPTER 2

"That you, Lonny? Midge?" Dad comes out of the workshop, wiping his hands on a rag. He's not big like me, but he's strong. All muscles and knuckles and knots. "You all right?" he says. "Where've you been?" He's still got his working specs on, thick as your thumb.

"We went all the—"

I give Midge a shove. He's such a snitch.

"We went looking for mushrooms," I say. "Morels. Couldn't find any, though." I hold out the basket. "Only ink caps."

Dad sticks the rag in his back pocket. "You've been a long time. How far did you go? You missed lunch."

"We're not hungry. Are we, Midge?"

Midge looks at me.

Course we're hungry. But if we eat now, there won't be any food left for dinner.

Dad flips his lenses up and rubs his eyes. "How far did you go?"

"It's fine, Dad," I tell him. "Don't worry, we never go past the oaks."

Midge stares at the floor. Keep quiet, tattle-teller.

"Good. Make sure you don't." Dad takes the basket from me. "What happened to your boots? They're soaked."

I scrunch up my toes. "We just … fell into the stream. That's all."

"Both of you?"

"Both of us."

Midge nods.

"Well, you'd better take more care next time – new boots are the last thing we can afford. Lonny, there's some old newspapers in the back of the workshop – stuff them with those and they'll keep a bit of shape while they're drying. Midge, I need your help with these watches. We've got to get them finished."

Midge pulls off his boots and slips behind Dad into the workshop.

"I can help too," I say. "With the watches. If you're in a hurry with them."

Dad rubs the stubble on his chin. "No. S'all right, Lon."

Course he doesn't want your help, Lonny. Your ham-fisted, unhelpful help.

He holds up the basket. "Good job on these, though. They'll go lovely with some eggs for dinner. Who needs morels?" He puts it on the kitchen table. "You get on with stuffing those boots. Chickens need sorting too, don't forget."

Boot stuffing and chicken sorting. Great.

I follow him into the workshop. Midge is already perched at the bench. He's surrounded by shelves and shelves of watchmaking equipment: scales and monitors and gear-pullers and dust-blowers and balance wheels and pivot lathes. Backs of watches and fronts of watches. Winding stems for the sides of watches. Cogs and springs and screws so little that some of them are completely invisible if all you've got is your bare human eyes.

Midge is calm in here. Happy. His fretting's all gone. Ignore the cap and he looks like nothing more in the world than a smaller version of Dad. The same concentrated face; the same hunched shoulders; the same careful hands.

I turn over my own hands. Straighten my fingers. Big. Wide. Clumsy.

Boot-stuffing, chicken-sorting hands.

They're magic too, though, don't forget. *Life-giving.*

For the fat lot of good it does me.

I pull the box of newspapers down from the shelf.

Dad opens up the dark wooden case where he stores watches while they're half-made, or half-mended. He covers his hand with a cloth and lifts out a perfectly round, almost-finished, 44-millimetre lever-set pocket watch. His speciality.

He passes it to Midge.

The watch gleams. It's made the old-fashioned way, with seventeen jewels, just like the classic pocket watches made a hundred years ago. When it's finished it'll have a fine leather fob looped round the top and Just-the-Job Jess will pick it up and take it into the city. You'll be able to buy it from Everston's the Jeweller and it won't lose or gain more than two seconds per year guaranteed. And when it does finally gallop ahead or fall behind, you can send it back through Everston's, and Dad and Midge'll tweak it till it's perfect all over again.

Trouble is, there's not much demand for pocket watches nowadays.

That's why we have to make ours the best, says Dad.

I take the top newspaper out of the box. My hungry stomach growls.

Dad lifts out a second watch and flips his lenses down. He twists a flat palm over the watch and the back comes off neatly. He nods to Midge, who does the same.

He places the back piece into a plastic tray. Midge does the same.

Everything you take off has to go into the tray, so it

doesn't get lost.

BANG! BANG!

The ceiling shudders. Dad sighs.

BANG! BANG! BANG!

It's Grandad upstairs, banging his walking stick on the floor. Dad keeps threatening to take it away if he doesn't stop. Says he'll give him a little brass bell instead. But Grandad said *bells are for churches and angels and old-fangled doorways and they aren't much assistance when you're trying to get across the landing to spend a periwinkle, thank you very much.*

"S'GONE FOUR!" shouts Grandad. "WHAT'RE YOU ALL DOODLING AWAY AT DOWN THERE? WHERE'S MY CUPPA?"

BANG! BANG! BANG!

"WHERE'S MY CUPPA?"

Dad squeezes his eyes shut and takes a deep breath in through his nose. "Lonny," he says, "make your grandad a cup of tea, will you? We've got to get these watches finished. Jess is coming to collect them in the morning."

"Here you go, Grandad." I push his creaking bedroom door open. The cup of tea – made with our very last drop of milk – slooshes in the mug.

"Lonny! Marvellous." Grandad's sitting on the bed. The room smells of shelves that haven't been dusted enough and floors that haven't been hoovered enough. "Grand old duke of a job." He pats the bed beside him. "Have a little sittle down, eh? Or would you prefer the chair? More comfy? I can move my stuff off if you like." He fumbles for his stick and begins to creak himself to upright.

"No, Grandad – don't get up. I've got to go and sort the chickens."

I can't stay here in this stuffy old-person room.

"But, Lon, I thought we could have a heave-ho on the old draughts board. Let you go first? Or d'you wanna look at Grandma Quicke's exercise book? S'been a while since you read any of her stories."

"I've gotta go, Grandad. I'll leave this here, all right?"

I put the tea down on the bedside table and dodge back out the door.

CHAPTER 3

A tale from Grandma Quicke's exercise book

I'm going to tell you a story. A true story. From way, way back in the days before cars or lorries or aeroplanes, when everyone went around on juddering pushbikes or snorting, stamping ponies and you had to wind your wristwatch up every single day or you'd get lost in time.

Way back then – lots and lots of greats ago – lived your great-great-great-great-great-great-great-great-grandmother. Her name was Lucy Cooper, and she lived in the town of Farstoke, far away from anywhere else in the world.

Farstoke had been there for as long as anyone could remember, and a lot longer than that, no doubt. It had a Northgate, a Southgate, an Eastgate and a Westgate.

Just east of the Westgate stood a very large house, where Lucy worked as a scullery maid. It was called Sinkly Manor, having been occupied by the Sinkly family for a very long time indeed. Made their money from buttons, the Sinklys did. You could make money from things like that in those days. And if you think about it, buttons are very useful. Especially before zips came along.

Anyway, the young gentleman of the house, Mr Louis Edward Sinkly, had an eye for the young ladies and he took quite a fancy to our Lucy. But Lucy had a little more self-respect than to allow a gentleman of the house to kiss her in the pantry, so she spurned his advances. In any case, Lucy was in love with the watchmaker's son, a quiet boy with not much money but a fine heart and good boots, and that would do very nicely as far as she was concerned.

In time, your great-great-great-great-great-great-great-great-grandmother came to marry the watchmaker's son, and she was able to leave Sinkly Manor, and she had two sweet baby boys. They named the first Isaac, and the second Daniel. And Mr Louis Edward Sinkly married a lady by the name of Freida, poor lass. It's told she was forced into the union by her father, and that she died an early death. But that's by the by. What matters for this story is that

Louis and Freida had two little babies themselves, Gordon and Gordana, innocent babes who grew up to be nasty spoilt little children, just like their father.

As for Lucy, it soon became apparent that one of her boys, Daniel, was a lifeling. He'd crawl for dying spiders in the corner of a room and bring them back to life, and cry like a teether when a kitten runt was perishing. Before long he was taller than his older brother. Lucy's husband, now the Farstoke watchmaker for his father had died of old age, confessed that there had indeed been incidents of lifelings in the family line. He said they must keep it quiet and no one must know, for non-lifeling folk have a terrible tendency to treat lifelings with appalling disregard.

So Lucy took it upon herself to keep her son safe, teaching him how to keep his special gift a secret and how to use it sparingly, or all his life would be gone before he knew it.

Meanwhile, Mr Louis Edward Sinkly, grown bored of his own poor wife, took to spying on Lucy, watching her hang laundry through the bushes, or knead bread through the window. And one day he got right up close while she was talking to her not-so-little Daniel, and he discovered her secret – that Daniel was a lifeling.

He waited until the watchmaker was out of town on business one day and Lucy was alone. He confronted her. He would tell everyone in Farstoke Daniel's secret, he said, unless she left her husband

and agreed to return to Sinkly Manor. Poor Lucy. She was about to agree to his unreasonable demand (for what else could she do?) when she was saved at the last moment by a terrible scream. Or so she thought. Sadly things would not work out well for poor Lucy and her family, but one thing at a time. I'll get back to the scream.

It wasn't Lucy screaming, or either of her sweet sons. No. It was the spoilt Gordana, all frills and curls and patent shoes. The foolish child had poked at a snake's nest just beyond the Westgate, and now her brother, Gordon, was near death, having been bitten by a terrified adder.

Gordana's scream shook your heart and rattled your ear bones. Louis Edward ran to her aid, and so did poor Freida. Once they'd calmed the girl down sufficiently to understand what had happened, her father knew exactly what action he'd take. He rushed to the watchmaker's house, took dear Daniel by the arm and pulled him out into the street. And Daniel got the buzzing.

The closer to Gordon he was dragged, the stronger the buzzing became.

Lucy chased after them but to no avail. Louis Edward was strong from fencing and horsemanship – he just pushed her aside. And, in any case, the buzzing is powerful when a human child's life is in question. It's all but irresistible. Daniel was drawn to Gordon not only by the hand of Mr Sinkly, but by his own lifeling urges.

He needed to be taken away, for his own good, for his own preservation – but all Mr Sinkly did was drag him closer.

They reached the swollen, weak Gordon – about to perish at any moment.

There was no option – the buzzing was strong, death was near. Daniel touched the boy's cheek and the life flowed through – out of Daniel, into Gordon.

And all was calm.

All except Lucy.

She threw herself past Freida, past Gordana, past Louis. She grabbed her son, held him at arm's length so she could see him proper.

The boy was gone.

In his place was an old, wrinkled man. Her son. She hugged him close.

Mr Sinkly lifted his own son in his arms and carried him back home with not a second look at Lucy or Daniel. Not a second look.

And that's why we live in the forest now. To keep our lifelings safe.

CHAPTER 4

I squeeze my feet into too-tight wellies and trudge down to the chickens, carrying the egg basket, the bucket, the broom and a sackful of straw.

The coop's down the bottom of the garden. It's half covered and half not, and it sits inside a huge run topped and sided with chicken wire, so every afternoon they all get out for a good bit of grass-pecking time. The rest of the garden hasn't got a fence – it just turns into forest at the edges. *Not much point in fences*, says Dad. *Only things fences keep out are people, and people don't hang round for long once Grandad starts hollering out of the window.*

I step into the run and shut the gate good and sure

behind me.

Chuck, chuck, chuck, chuck, chuck. The chickens blink at me through the coop wire.

"I haven't got any food. I've come to let you out for a run. Like I've done every afternoon since forever." I slide up the hatch and they run out – Dixon first – then one, two, three, four, five red hens. Only five?

Crock-a-crock-a-crock! Dixon crows at me.

"Where's Layla?" I ask him.

Six pairs of eyes all look up at me, heads bobbing.

Chuck, chuck, chuck, chuck, chuck.

"I haven't got any food." You'd think they were starved, and there wasn't a full litre of seed topped up in the feeder just this morning and a bowl of mash put out in the coop. They eat better than us and I'm not even exaggerating. "Go on, go look for worms. I need to find Layla."

I unlatch the coop door and climb inside. Lift the lids off the laying boxes and peep in. There she is. Gone broody again. Least that should mean there's another egg under there with a bit of luck.

"Come on, girl." I go to pick her up.

She pecks me.

"I know, I'm sorry." I stroke the side of her head, just behind her eye. "We need the eggs, though. We really do." Her eyelids droop. Her head gets heavy. She lets me lift her off. "That's it. Good girl."

And there it is. A smooth brown egg. Fresh as anything.

Knew they'd start to lay a few more now spring's properly here.

"Clever girl, Layla. Clever girl." I hold her to my chest, wings tucked tight. Her feathers make her look fat and sturdy, but when you've got her in your hands you can feel her narrow bones. I kiss the top of her head. She rumbles a quiet cluck.

"Good girl." I put her on the ground and she's off to find the others.

I pick up the warm egg, put it safe in my basket, and start on sweeping up the floor.

We must've got nearly to Farstoke earlier.

"Farstoke." I say it out loud.

It sits in my throat.

It sucks out my breath.

I pull out the old straw from the laying boxes and shove it into the bucket for compost. Take the scraper out of my pocket and work the dried chicken gunk off the perch.

Farstoke. It's got a clock tower in the centre and four city gates. Each gate is topped with a statue.

The Northgate has a stag in full antler. I've got a photograph of it. With my mother standing underneath. Smiling in the sunshine.

I've got other photographs, too.

I put fistfuls of fresh straw into the laying boxes, then gather up the broom and the bucket and the basket and the sack. I take them all out into the run. The chickens peck and fuss and bicker.

Hold on – what was that?

A flash of orange, down the end of the garden. Between the trees.

Crock-a-crock-a-crock!

Not those girls again – Erin and Katy?

It couldn't be, could it?

Crock-a-crock-a-crock!

I squint at the shade between the birches.

You're going crazy, Lonny. There's no way they'd come this far. You're fretting. Worse than Midge.

There – again – a flash of orange.

Crock-a-crock-a-crock!

"FOX!"

Grandad? I look back to the house.

"FOX!" He's looking down the garden through his binoculars, elbows hanging out the window. "GET AWAY, YOU BUSHY-BOTTOMED BLIGHTER! GET AWAY!"

Fox.

Course it is.

It's not the girls at all. Course it's not.

A quick nose, a disappearing tail, and the fox is gone. Not that it had anything to fear from Grandad. It's been a good year since he even bothered making it downstairs, let alone into the garden. He's no threat to anyone.

Fox doesn't know that, though.

"S'all right, Grandad," I shout up. "It's gone."

"IT'S WHAT?"

His legs won't hold him up, his ears don't work so good and he hasn't had his own teeth since the Saxon times or something, but the thing about Grandad is his voicebox has discovered the secret of everlasting youth. *He'll be yelling at us from his grave*, Dad says.

"Gone, Grandad. It's gone."

"GONE?" He creaks himself round so his binoculars are pointing right at me. "DON'T YOU BELIEVE IT, LONNY. CUNNING LITTLE FUGGLES THEY ARE. TWO SNIFFS OF A CHICKEN'S WING TIP AND THERE'S TROUBLE ON YOUR DOORSTEP FOR THE FORESEEABLE."

Vmmmmm

A tingle on the right side of my top lip.

I press it. Try to squash it away.

"MAKE DOUBLE-CHECKERED SURE YOU SHUT THAT CHICKENY GATE WHEN YOU'RE DONE."

Vmmmmmmmm

The tingle spreads through my cheek into my jaw.

"I will, Grandad," I call up. "Don't worry."

Vmmmmmmmmmm

In the roof of my mouth. In the deep of my ears. The buzzing.

Vmmmmmmmmmmmm

Tiny.

Faint.

Hardly there at all.

Vmmmmmmmmmmmmmm

Something's dying.

Something very small.

Something that barely had any life to begin with.

Vmmmmmmmmmmmmmmmmmmm

I close my eyes. Feel where it's coming from.

Vmmmmmmmmmmmmmmmmmmmm

There. On the ground.

A moth.

Maybe it's been pecked by a chicken. Or stood on by a too-tight boot.

I kneel down.

It's on its side. A brimstone – female, I reckon. Bright-yellow wings with brown edges, like she's flown too close to a flame.

She waves an antenna. Shudders a scorched silky wing.

Not long now and she'll be dead.

Walk away?

I could.

It wouldn't be hard.

It's a moth, though. What difference will it make? A few seconds of my life maybe, for the whole rest of hers.

I glance up at Grandad. His binoculars are back on the forest.

I drop the broom and the bucket and the basket and the sack. Hover my hand above the dying brimstone.

Burnt edges.

Broken wings.

Millimetres away from my fingertips.

Walk away.

I close my fist and stand up.

What am I thinking? I already saved a rabbit today. If I carry on at this rate, there'll be nothing left. I'll end up stuck upstairs, doddery as Grandad. I grab the things and trudge back to the house, stuff piled up in my arms and stuff piled up in my mind.

I check round the workshop door. It's OK. Midge is still there with Dad, specs on and eyes focused. I scoot upstairs to our room, scramble over Midge's bed and on to mine. I slide my hand between the mattress and the bed frame.

Where is it?

I wiggle my hand further in. The old springs scratch at my fingers.

There.

Mum's photograph album.

Its red marbled cover is split along the spine and the plastic sheets over the pictures have gone stiff and yellow. Some of the photos have come unstuck so now they just sit between the pages and you have to take care they don't fall out. And Mum's handwriting – where she's written the place name of every single photo – has faded and furred and fuzzed round the edges. But it's my most precious thing in the world. And no one else knows I've got it.

I found it in Dad's wardrobe. Ages ago. Under a

pile of Mum's things. Clothes and bags and boots and books. He never touches it, not any of it. It all just stays there in the same-shaped heap year after year.

So I reckoned he wouldn't mind if I had this. Or I reckoned he wouldn't notice, more like.

I'll start on the first page, just like I always do. Even though I know every detail of it already. Even though I could hide it back under the mattress and close my eyes and still list off every single picture in the exact right order with the exact right words that go next to it.

I'll go through them one by one. I never skip, or start in the middle, or flip to the back. Every picture is just as important as the one before it, and the one after.

I open the cover.

She's standing in front of a whole row of higgledy-piggledy, squished-up houses – all pink and blue and white. She's got on a black woolly hat and a scarf the colour of almost-ripe raspberries. Her coat's zipped all the way up and there's snow on the squished-up rooftops. Her raspberry scarf has little white hoops dotted all over it.

Golden Lane, Prague. Her handwriting's short and round, like all the letters want to be "o"s, even the "l"s and the "r"s and the "g"s.

Prague.

My map of the world is stuck up on the wall above the head of my bed. I lay the album down and stand on my pillow. The springs moan. *Doing. Creeeaaaak. Doing.*

There it is. *Prague.* Circled faintly in pencil. North of Bohemia, south of Dresden. Just to the east of the sticky-taped tear.

Wonder if I'll ever get there.

Wonder if I'll ever stand where she stood in Golden Lane.

I won't if Dad has anything to do with it. If Dad has anything to do with it, I'll never even get beyond the blinkin' oaks.

The next photograph has slipped and got wedged where the pages meet. I ease it out.

Mum's standing bare-armed in the brightness. She's with three other people. Behind them is the grandest building – grander than anything you could ever think up. It's got rows and rows of arched windows and rows and rows of rectangular windows and lots of statues standing all along the top of it. The whole thing glows peachy and amber in the sunshine.

The Palace of Versailles, France.

The front bit of her hair is drawn back and fixed into place with a slide. Her eyelids are dark with make-up.

I stand up. *Doing. Creeeeak. Doing.* Find France on the map. Versailles is there, circled faintly and hugged in next to Paris.

The next page is *Edinburgh Castle.*

She's wearing the raspberry scarf again. And brown knitted gloves. The front bit of her hair's escaped from its slide and blown across her face.

After that there's the *Tower of London*, *St Paul's Cathedral*, the *Trevi Fountain*, the *Acropolis*.

The last four photographs are of Farstoke – one at each gate. All taken on the same day, I reckon. It's bright. Sunny. A clear sky. She's wearing the same clothes in all four. That raspberry scarf still wrapped round her neck, even though it wasn't cold from the look of it.

First one's the Northgate. Stag on top, my mother underneath. Smiling. Her T-shirt's dark green, with four white capital letters across the front. *LIFE*.

I looked for it once – the *LIFE* T-shirt. I looked for her coat too, and her black woolly hat, and her gloves, and her scarf. Searched through Dad's wardrobe. I found the hat and the gloves, the exact same ones. I held them against my cheeks, breathed them in. But they just smelled old and dusty. I left them in the wardrobe.

Crock! Crock! Crock-a-crock!

Dixon?

What's he crowing about?

Trying to impress the hens, I s'pose.

I turn over the page.

Eastgate. The hang-shouldered wolf. My mother looks up at it. Pulls a pretend-scared face.

Crock! Crooooooock!

Oh, be quiet, Dixon. Stop showing off.

Next page is the Westgate.

Crock-a-crock!

She's brushing her hair away from her face in this one. Eyes closed, lips squeezed together. The bear rears up above her.

Crock! Crock! Crock!

What on earth's going on out there? Hold on, Dixon, I'll be out in a minute.

The very last page of the album – it's the Southgate, with its goose.

She's with another friend in this one. They're sharing the scarf, heads tilted towards each other. Both smiling. Both squinting in the sunshine. That same T-shirt. *LIFE.*

Crock-a-crock-a-crooooooooock!

Oh, Dixon. All right, all right, I'm—

"FOX!" It's Grandad.

BANG! BANG! BANG!

He bashes his stick on the floorboards.

BANG! BANG! BANG!

"FOX!" His super-voice bellows through the house. "FOX IN THE CHICKEN RUN! FOX IN THE CHICKEN RUN!"

Fox in the run?

But I closed the gate.

Didn't I?

CHAPTER 5

I slam the album shut, shove it under the mattress.

BANG! BANG! BANG!

"FOX!"

Vmmmmmmmm

The edge of my lip.

The flesh of my cheek.

Maybe it's not the buzzing.

Maybe it's not.

I dive across the bedroom and leap down the stairs four at a time.

Dad's already skidding towards the back door. "Damn it," he says. He shoves his feet into his shoes and stumbles outside.

Vmmmmmmmmmmmm

Midge is pulling soggy newspaper out of his drying boots. I push him aside and run into the garden in my socks.

Vmmmmmmmmmmmmmmm

One of them's dying. One of the chickens.

VMMMMMMMMMMMMMMMM

There's another.

Thrmmmmmmmmmmm

And another.

Vmmmmmmmmmmmmmmmmmmmmm

And another.

Four buzzings? Five? Six? Can't count them. My head whirls.

I trip over, flat on my chest.

Thrmmmmmmmmm

Vmmmmmmmmmmmm

VMMMMMMMMMMMM

Vmmmmmmmmmmmmmmmmmmmmm

I scrabble to my knees.

My tongue, my head, my lips, my throat – they pull me towards the coop.

I get to my feet.

Got to reach the chickens. Got to help them.

I reach the run, duck in through the open gate.

"Get away!" Dad roars from inside the coop. "Get away!"

VMMMMMMMMMMMMMMMMMMMMM

The fox scampers out, a limp hen hanging from its

mouth. It slips past me and bolts into the forest.

Vmmmmmmmmmmmmmmmmmmmmmmmmmmm

I stagger into the coop.

"Get away! Get away!" Dad roars again.

Vmmmmmmmmmmmmmmmmmmmmmmmmmmm

Thrrmmmmmmmmmmmmmmmmmmmmmmmmm

VMMMMMMMMMMMMMMMMMMMMM

Don't know where to go first.

Twitching heads.

Curling feet.

Flapping wings.

"I said get away!"

"It's all right." It's Midge. He's close behind me. "The fox has gone, Dad. It ran into the forest."

"Not the fox!" Dad roars louder. "*Lonny!* We have to get Lonny out!"

VMMMMMMMMMMMMMMMMMMMMM

It's Dixon. On his side.

He blinks. *Blink. Blink. Blink.*

Vmmmmmmmmmmmmmmmmmmmmmmmmmmm

Monica. Wings wide. Foot jerking.

Vmmmmmmmmmmmmmmmmmmmmmmmmmmm

Layla.

My Layla.

I drop down to the floor, fold her into my arms.

"Lonny." Dad quietens his voice. "You've got to walk away."

Vmmmmmmmmmmmmmmmmmmmmmmmmmmm

The buzzing snakes through my arms.

Dad pulls at my shoulders. "Walk away, Lonny. Walk away."

But we're fixed together, me and Layla. We're fixed firm. And the buzzing flows like blood, out of my fingers into her bones and her flesh and her feathers.

"*Chuck*," she says. Ever so quiet. Ever so soft. "*Chuck*."

She's back.

I unwrap my exhausted arms.

She shakes herself. She's as dazed as me.

VMMMMMMMMMMMMMMMMMMMMMMM

Vmmmmmmmmmmmmmmmmmmmmmmmmmmmm

Thrmmmmmmmmmmmmmmmmmmmmmmmmmmmm

Dad grips me under my armpits. He pulls me up, lifts me to my feet, even though I'm taller than him.

I've got to help the others.

VMMMMMMMMMMMMMMMMMMMMMMMMMM

Dad's head is close. "Time to walk away now," he whispers, good and firm.

Walk away.

Walk away.

"Midge," he says, "move those birds."

"But where shall I—"

"Just move them! As far away as you can."

"But there's blood and they're not al—"

"Just take them away, Midge!"

"But they're not all dead ye—"

"Now! Right now!"

Vmmmmmmmmmmmmmmmmmmmmmmmmmmmm

37

Thrmmmmmmmmmmmmmmmmmmmmmmmmmmmm
I open my mouth. Shift my jaw side to side.

Midge grabs the mauled chickens – three? Four? Five? Takes them out of the run, down towards the trees.

VMMMMMMMMMMMMMMMMMMMMMM
Vmmmmmmmmmmmmmmmmmmmmmmmmmmm
Thrmmmmmmmmmmmmmmmmmmmmmmmmmm.

I press the sides of my head. Dad puts his hands over mine. Warm, watchmaking hands.

I close my eyes. "I'm going to be sick."

"That's all right."

I'm not sick, though. It doesn't come out. It just sits in my stomach.

"C'mon," says Dad. "We'll walk away together. Back to the house."

We step out of the coop, my head still in my hands.

VMMMMMMMMMMMMMMMMMMMMMM
Vmmmmmmmmmmmmmmmmmmmmmmmmmmm
Thrmmmmmmmmmmmmmmmmmmmmmmmmmm

"Take them further, Midge," shouts Dad. "Further the better."

"But some of them are—"

"We'll deal with them soon as we can."

The buzzings pull me backward. But Dad's there, hands on my shoulders. Pushing me forward. "Walk away, Lonny," he says. "Walk away."

I put my right foot in front.

Then my left.

Then my right.

Then my left.

VMMMMMMMMMMMMMMMMMMMMMMMM

Vmmmmmmmmmmmmmmmmmmmmmmmmmmm

Thrmmmmmmmmmmmmmmmmmmmmmmmmmm

If I keep putting one foot forward, and then another, I'll get there.

Walk away.

Walk away.

Right.

Left.

Right.

Left.

VMMMMMMMMMMMMMMMMMMMMMMMM

Vmmmmmmmmmmmmmmmmmmmmmmmmmmm

I stop. "What about the eggs?"

Thrmmmmmmmmmmmmmmmmmmmmmmmmmm

"What?" says Dad.

"If the chickens all die, what are we going to eat?"

"Layla's alive. Keep walking."

"That's not enough."

"I promised your mother I wouldn't let you waste your life away. I promised her." There's a clog in his voice. "And those watches are nearly done. Jess is coming to pick them up first thing. We'll have money soon. So just forget the stupid chickens and keep walking."

Left.

Right.

Left.
Right.
VVVMMMMMMMMMMMMMMMMMMMMMMMMM
Thrmmmmmmmmmmmmmmmmmmmmmmmmmmmmm
The buzzings weaken.
Keep walking, Lonny. Keep walking.
Dad takes me in the house. He steers me up the stairs and into Grandad's room.

CHAPTER 6

Grandad's in the chair by the window, binoculars in his hands, tears smudged down his cheeks. "Dixon?" he says. "Did it get Dixon?"

Dad pushes me inside. "Look after him, will you?"

I'm not sure which of us he's talking to.

He closes the door behind him.

"A lot of birds been got out there." Grandad puts down his binoculars. Rubs his wet face. "Harsh amount of buzzing for lifeling boy."

The room's hot and stuffy and smelly. Just like always. I lie down on the hot, stuffy, smelly bed. Curl myself up in the hot, stuffy, smelly sheets.

Vmmmmmmmmmmmmmmm

Thrmmmmmmmmmmm

Grandad pushes himself up from his chair and shuffles to the door. His slippers *shush-ush-ush* on the floorboards. He turns the key in the lock. "Putting this little key-ma-jig in my pocket," he says. "Just for certainty's sake."

I press my knuckles into my forehead. "I hate foxes. I hate them."

Grandad sits on the edge of the bed. "Fox was just doing what it knew best. Trying to take care of its family." He puts a hand on my arm. A papery, trembly, ancient hand. "Can't blame the fox."

I blame it. I blame it completely one hundred per cent.

If I don't blame the fox, there's only one other person whose fault it can be.

There's a bright, sharp outline all round our bedroom door. Thought Midge'd be asleep by now but he hasn't turned the light out yet.

I go in. There's a scrabbling over the far side of the room – *my* side of the room.

"Midge? What're you doing?"

He's crouched on the floor. Got something wrapped in his arms, trying to hide it.

"What's that?"

It's something red. Something marbled.

"That's mine!" I leap over the bed but he ducks out of the way, taking the album with him.

He squeezes it tight.

"Give it back."

"I only want to look at it," he says. "It was sticking out from under your mattress. I wondered what it was. I just want to—"

"Give it to me." I jump back over the bed but he's quick, Midge is. He shoots out the door.

"It's mine!" I scramble after him, on to the landing, down the stairs.

"No, it's not – it's Mum's." He trips on the bottom stair in the dimness but keeps himself up with the handrail.

"*My* mum's," I shout.

He swings round towards the workshop.

Don't even think about it, Midge. Don't even thinking about showing that to Dad.

"Mine too!" He crashes through the doorway.

Dad stands up. "Midge! Lonny! Be careful!"

We bash into the worktable.

"You never even knew her!"

"Lonny!" says Dad. "Stop!"

"Dad! Look!" Midge skids round the back of the room and up the other side so the worktable's in between us. "He's got these photos – he's been keeping them secret."

Snitch.

Tattle-teller.

My chest and fists and teeth tremble.

I want to get him.

I want to kill him.

"I only want to look at them." He hugs the album closer.

My album.

My pictures.

My mother.

"If it weren't for you," I said, "she'd still be alive."

"Lonny!"

I dive across the worktable and grab at the album. I knock it out of his hands and slide straight into the wooden box.

The wooden box with the two perfect almost-ready pocket watches inside.

It spins away. I make a grab for it.

CRASH!

It smashes to the floor. Watch pieces scatter.

I fall off the edge of the table, knocking the plastic trays flying. I bash into Dad's stool. It tips over on to the open, broken box.

I look at the floor. Two perfect watches in a thousand messed-up bits.

Dad grasps at the tiny pieces.

Backs and fronts and hands and springs and screws.

"I can help." I gather up some bits that have rolled under the table. "We can fix them. All of us together – we can fix them."

Midge stands glued against the wall. Not even helping.

Dad stops. Stands up. Closes his eyes.

"Dad?" I say. "We can fix them. We can. If we all help."

His shoulders lift with each breath.

"Dad?"

He opens his hands and lets the watch pieces tumble to the floor.

He takes off his working specs, closes the arms carefully, one at a time, and places them on the table. He picks up the photograph album and opens the first page. *Golden Lane.*

Then the second. *The Palace of Versailles.*

"One day," I say, "I'm going to go to all the places she went to. All the places in those photographs."

He keeps turning the pages.

Edinburgh Castle.

The Tower of London.

Midge watches him. "What was she like?" he says.

Dad closes the album and clutches it to his chest. It's facing back side out. I can see the top, where Mum wrote her name in thick faded pen. *Maria Kemp.*

Dad leaves the workshop, still clutching the album. His feet *clomp clomp clomp* on the stairs.

Bang! He slams his bedroom door.

And all that's left is the slow and steady *tock tock tock* of the grandfather clock in the corner of the room.

"What was she like?" says Midge again.

What was she like?

I don't know, do I?

I barely remember anything. Just a blur of hair, a turning head. I've got hardly anything at all. Just the edges of memories and a bunch of old photographs. The rest has slipped between my fingers. I should've held on tighter.

Midge blinks. Annoying tiny tears in his annoying tiny eyes.

Even if I did remember, I wouldn't tell him.

I mean, they go to hospital for Midge to be born, and she doesn't come back. Only Dad comes back, with a squealing, squirming baby Midge.

No more Mum.

No more kisses and kind words.

Midge hasn't moved. Hasn't even tried to pick any of the pieces up off the floor. Calls himself a watchmaker?

"This is all your fault," I say. "All of it. Everything."

CHAPTER 7

DING-DONG!

Mmmm?

DING-DONG!

What's that?

I stick my head out from under the bedsheets.

DING-DONG!

What's the time? What's going on? I always get woken up by Dix—

Oh.

Dixon.

DING-DONG!

"Lonny! Lonny!" Midge scampers into the room. "It's Jess! She's at the door. I think she saw me."

"What?" I fling off the sheets and rush to the window.

"Lonny! Don't! She'll see you too!"

There's Jess's massive van parked on the gravel, with its tatty beige curtains and its cardboard-and-felt-tip sign propped up in the back window.

Just-the-Job Jess
No Job Too Tiny
117 Sinkly Square, Farstoke

"Where's Dad?" I ask. "Why isn't he answering the door?"

DING-DONG!

"He won't get up," says Midge. "I can't get him out of bed. He's sick or something."

Sick? So sick he can't answer the door? Who else does he think is going to do it? Grandad's not getting down those stairs in a hurry and they've both taught me and Midge to hide from visitors ever since we were crawlers. *No exceptions.*

"DOORBELL'S RINGLING!" shouts Grandad.

Great. That's all we need.

He whacks his stick on the floor. *BANG! BANG! BANG!*

I pull on a pair of trousers and yank a T-shirt over my head. "Stay in here, Midge." I lope out on to the landing and knock on Dad's bedroom door.

No answer.

"The watches are all broken, Lonny." Midge pokes his head out of our room. "I tried to fix them but—"

"I said stay in there."

DING-DONG!

"Dad?" I push the door open. "You all right?" The curtains are still closed, but daylight has soaked through the thin material and washed the room pinkish. "Dad?"

"DOORBELL!"

The wardrobe door hangs wide. Mum's stuff has been pulled out, strewn over the floor. There's a Dad-shaped lump hunched in the bed, with its back towards me.

"Go away," it growls.

"But I think it's Jess – at the door. Come to pick up the watches."

"Ignore her. She'll go away."

"But what about the—"

"Leave me alone."

On the floor, right next to the bed, is the photo album. *My* photo album.

I s'pose maybe Dad needs it for a little while.

"Are you sure you're all right?" I ask him.

"I'm fine."

"But—"

"Go away." The Dad-shaped lump pulls its cover further over its head.

BANG! BANG! BANG!

"OK," I say. "OK."

I close the door.

"WHAT ON EARTH IS DOODLING ON WITH YOU LOT? NO ONE'S GETTING THE DOOR AND NO ONE'S FETCHED MY BREAKFAST! YOU PLANNING TO STARVE ME? YOU TRYING TO SHUFFLE ME INTO MY CASKET?"

"Course not, Grandad," I call from the hallway. "Midge? Hasn't Dad even got Grandad's breakfast yet?"

"I DON'T HAVE ANY MILLIONS YOU KNOW. I DON'T HAVE ANY BURROWED-AWAY TREASURES. THERE'S NOTHING TO BE GAINED FROM POLISHING ME OFF."

Midge sticks his head out again. "He's not been up. Not even once. And there isn't any food anyway. No milk and no bread and no eggs and no—"

Tap-tap-tap.

Midge freezes.

I peer down the stairs. It's Jess, tapping on the kitchen window.

"Hel-lo?" she calls. "Mr Quicke? Anyone home?"

"Lonny," says Midge. "You gotta hide."

Scrunch, scrunch, scrunch.

Jess's feet on the gravel. Trudging round the side of the house.

"What are we going to do?" Midge's eyes are welling up. Like crying's going to help the situation.

"Just wait," I tell him. "Just wait and she'll go away."

"Hel-lo? Hel-lo? It's Jess, Mr Quicke. Come to pick up your watches."

"QUIT YER HOLLERIN'!"

"Mr Quicke?"

"MR QUICKE THE ELDER AND IMPORTANTER, I THINK YOU'LL FIND. NOW QUIT YER HOLLERIN'. IT'S INTERRUPTING MY PEACE."

"Well, good morning, Mr Quicke the Elder! Long time no see. How are things with you?"

"I'D BE A HEAP OF A LOT BETTER IF MY PEACE WASN'T BEING SO RUDELY INTERRUPTED."

"I'm very sorry about that, Mr Quicke, but I promised your son I'd pick up his watches today. For Everston's. He's expecting me."

"WELL, IF HE'S NOT ANSWERING, I'D SAY IT'S A PRETTY GOOD GUESSTIMATE THAT HE NO LONGER REQUIRES YOUR ASSISTANCE."

"But it was all agreed and—"

"IN THAT CASE IT HAS EVIDENTIONALLY BEEN UNAGREED. SO THERE'S NO PROBLEM HERE AND NOTHING TO SEE! NOW KINDLY LEAVE THE PREMISES."

"I'd really rather you checked with your son before sending me on my way, Mr—"

"GOODBYE, DISTURBER OF THE CALM. GOODBYE!"

"All right, well, please tell *Mr Quicke the Younger* I'll be back again tomorrow. No extra charge. And can you ask him if he needs me to get him any groceries from—"

"GOODBYE!"

"OK, OK. I know when I'm not wanted."

Scrunch scrunch scrunch. Jess comes round to the front of the house. She squints through the kitchen window again. I duck back behind the banister.

BANG! BANG! BANG!

A sob bubbles up out of Midge. His tiny Midge face creases into folds of tears and snot. "I tried to fix the watches but I couldn't find all the—"

"WHERE'S MY BREAKFAST?"

BANG! BANG! BANG!

I squeeze my eyes shut tight. Is this how Dad feels every time Grandad starts banging?

"What are we going to get Grandad for breakfast?" says Midge. "And what are we going to have for lun—"

"Stop, Midge!" I say. "Just stop."

Midge goes quiet. He sniffs a dribble of snot back up his nose.

Scrunch, scrunch, scrunch, scrunch, scrunch.

I scoot into the bedroom and look out the window. Jess opens the door of her van. She's got boots on with tassels down the back. They swish as she swings herself into the seat.

Nine o'clock in the evening. Twilight's settling over the back garden but Layla still spots me coming. She struts over to the side of the pen and makes lonely clucks. I step in, scatter a bit of seed and let her peck at my boots for a bit.

"All right, Layla? You OK? Any eggs?"

I've already checked the laying boxes three times today. I know they'll be empty but I'll look again anyway. That's just the sort of thing you do when all anyone's eaten all day is watery porridge and a shared-out tin of mandarins that you found in the back of a drawer.

I check the boxes. Nothing.

Don't suppose you feel much like laying eggs when all your friends have been got by a fox. I pick her up, kiss her downy back, feel her skinny bones.

So, that's it, then. No food in the house.

And Midge hasn't managed to fix the blinkin' watches because we can't even find half the bits. And Jess'll be here in the morning just like she was today and all we can do is –

Hold on.

Jess.

Just-the-Job Jess.

A *job*. That's what I need.

Earn some money. Proper money. So we can eat. And we don't have to depend on pocket watches that nobody wants. Or gathered-up mushrooms. Or one lonely chicken.

Layla flaps as I set her back down on the coop floor.

Yeah. I'll speak to Jess. Tomorrow morning. I'll open up the front door bold as anything and I'll speak to her. Just like that.

And I'll show everyone these boot-stuffing hands aren't so useless after all.

CHAPTER 8

"Hello, um, Mrs … um…" My words don't come out quite as easy as I imagined them. "Hello, Mrs … um … Just-the-Job."

Jess stares up at me like I'm some kind of overgrown ghost in the doorway. "Well, I never," she says.

She takes a step forward on the gravel. *Scrunch.*

"Well, I never," she says again. "All the years I've been coming here and the only glimpse I've managed to get of you Quicke boys is the backs of your heels running up the stairs." She sticks out her arm. "Call me Jess." Her fingernails are bright orange.

Now I see her close up, she's older than I thought she was. Closer to Grandad's age than Dad's, for sure.

But she's nothing like Grandad. She doesn't dress old for a start. She's got jeans on and different boots from yesterday. They look like something you'd see in a cowboy film except they've got sparkling silver stones round the tops. Don't think our part of the forest has ever seen anything so glittery.

I shake her hand, like I've seen people do on TV.

"And what's your name," she says, "if you don't mind me asking?"

"Oh. I'm Lonny."

She smiles.

"Lonny Quicke," I add.

"Well, Lonny Quicke, I am very pleased to meet you indeed. I didn't manage to speak to your dad yesterday. Is he all right? Do you need any help?"

"Um, I, um…" *Job, Lonny. You need a job.* "Um, yes. I mean, no. I mean, Dad's fine, I think, he's just … he's just not feeling very well. And the watches aren't ready yet. So I was wondering … if I might be able to find a job. I was wondering if you could help me."

"A job?" Jess has got a big purple bag slung over her shoulder. It's got swishing tassels on it, just like yesterday's boots. She hitches it up.

"Or just some work," I say. "Anything at all. To earn some money. I need to buy groceries, see. The chickens have been got by a fox so there aren't any eggs. And we've run out of milk. And bread. And, well, pretty much everything else too. So I need to get some money, to buy food."

Jess tilts her head to one side. "You're big, aren't you? Bigger than I thought you'd be." She does a little frown. "Mind you, I suppose that could be handy. And I do have a lot on at the moment. Yes. I'm sure I could give you a job or two, Lonny Quicke."

"That's brilliant. Thank you, Mrs – I mean, *Jess*."

"You want to come now? If the watches aren't finished, there's no point in me going to Everston's today."

"Come now? Where?"

"Back to Farstoke. For the jobs. I can't bring them here."

"Oh." Farstoke? "No. I mean, yes." Of course I'll have to go to Farstoke. "Yes, I'd like to come now. I just need to—"

"As long as your dad doesn't mind, that is. I'm not sure he likes you mixing with—"

"He won't mind." He won't *know*, more like. Not until I've already left anyway. "I just need to get my rucksack."

"You're sure your dad'll be all right with this?"

"He'll be fine."

"Oh – one other thing, Lonny." Jess glances over my shoulder into the house.

"What's that?"

"It's just a thought," she says. "But what about that brother of yours? The little one. Smaller than you. I've seen him scurrying away when I ring your doorbell."

"Midge?"

"Yes. *Midge*." She smiles. "I thought perhaps he might like to come too? I've got lots of things that need doing, so I'm sure I could find him some work as well."

Midge? Who frets if he even goes out of sight of our chimney pots? "I'm not sure if—"

"In fact," she says, "come to think of it, I've got a job that would be particularly suited to him. It needs, er, small fingers. Sorting out some tiny things. It'd drive you crazy and I can't do it, my eyesight's shot to bits – but it would suit your brother perfectly."

"Oh. Right."

And actually, why shouldn't Midge come too? Why shouldn't he earn some money to help feed us all? It's his fault the watches are broken. "All right," I say. "Yeah. All right. I'll go and get him. We'll both come to Farstoke."

"Splendid! Well, I'll be waiting in Celia."

"Celia?"

She nods towards the van. "My caravanette. And I hope you like country music, Lonny Quicke. The radio's tuned to Country Hits, and woe betide anyone who tries to retune it." She throws me a wink, turns round and scrunches back across the gravel, purple tassels swinging from her bag and boot jewels glinting in the sunshine.

I run upstairs to the bedroom. "Get your coat on," I tell Midge. "We're going to Farstoke."

He blinks. "Who is?"

"Me and you. Right now."

"But we can't."

"Yes, we can. Jess is here – she's waiting outside – and she's got a job for you."

"But—"

"This whole thing is your fault, Midge, so you're coming whether you like it or not. We have to earn some money and buy some food. Or everyone'll starve."

"But what if they find out about you?"

"They won't, OK? They won't, because we're not going to tell them."

"But what if they guess?"

I lunge across the bed and grab a scrunch of his shirt. "They're not going to guess. We're going to keep it secret, all right?" I yank him forward. "If you tell anyone – *anyone*, I swear I'll—"

"I won't! I won't!" A fat tear rolls down his cheek. It drips on to my fist.

He's so small. I could break him, just like that. Break him in two, I reckon.

I drop him down. "Listen," I tell him, "if anyone says anything about lifelings, you say *nothing*, all right? *Nothing*."

When we get outside Jess is grinning out of the van's open window. "Midge Quicke," she says. "What a pleasure. I've been waiting to meet you for such a long time. Nice hat."

I push Midge over to the door on the other side and

twist his stupid yellow cap the right way round on his head.

He changes it straight back again.

"Come on." Jess shoves some stuff off the seat. "Hop inside. Midge – meet Celia, my caravanette. Celia – this is Midge."

I shove him into the van.

Jess pats the seat beside her. "Sit in the middle between me and your brother."

I chuck my rucksack into the footwell and climb in after him.

Midge sits frozen. Can't he even try and act normal? I pull his seatbelt out and hold it in front of his face. He gets the message and takes it off me.

I clear my throat. "Ahem." Got to say something. Got to try and seem relaxed. I fiddle around behind me for my own seatbelt. "Why is your – um – why is your van – I mean, your *caravanette* – called Celia?"

"Why?" Jess turns the key and the van splutters into life. "My Ken named her. He bought her a couple of months before he died. Plan was, he'd do her up and we'd travel together. See the world. Never happened, of course."

"Oh. I'm sorry."

"No need to be sorry, Lonny. That's life, isn't it? Sometimes things just don't work out how you plan them." Jess sighs, then she pushes the gear stick forward. "Other times, though, a miracle drops down straight out of nowhere – isn't that right, Midge?"

She gives the back-to-front peak of Midge's cap a little tug. "And all we have to do is be there with our sleeves rolled up, nice 'n' ready to catch it. So, you both sorted now? Ready to go?"

"Yeah." My heart's walloping blood around my veins. "We're ready."

Jess drives Celia slowly across the gravel, away from our house, and out towards Farstoke.

Air.

I need more air.

There's an old-fashioned handle in the door to wind down the window. I get hold of it but it comes clean off in my ham-fisted, boot-stuffing hand.

Midge stares at it. Whips his head from me to Jess and back again.

Jess chuckles. "Don't worry, Lonny. Happens all the time. I've just about kept the old girl on the road but I never seem to have the time to get her properly finished. Just stick it back in again if you can."

I poke the handle back into the hole it came out of.

"Now, how about some music?" says Jess, fiddling with the knobs on the dashboard. "Oh, and I've got pear drops in the glove compartment. You ever had a pear drop, Midge? No? You're gonna love 'em."

CHAPTER 9

The edge of the forest. The edge of our world.

We drive out across a broad field, soft and white like overboiled milk. The road curls through it and the river chases alongside to the west, twice as wide and twice as fast as it is in the forest.

"*I'm broke, you're broke, we're both broken-hearted!*" Jess sings along to the radio while me and Midge stare out of the windows.

"What *is* all that white stuff?" I say.

"Dandelions," says Jess. "Gone to seed. Just in time for the festi—"

"Oh, look. There." I spot a town on the far side of the field. "Is that Farstoke?" There's a high grey stone

wall round it, with a tumble of rooftops peeping over the top.

"Yup. That's Farstoke," says Jess. "That's home."

I can make out a narrow building in the middle, higher than everything else. The clock tower.

And there, right where our road is headed – a huge, antlered stag.

We're close now. So close. The stag is massive against the blue wisped sky. Head lifted, antlers poised. Guarding his town.

We drive underneath. Right over where my mother stood in her raspberry scarf and her *LIFE* T-shirt.

Jess rolls her window down. The river gurgles and gallops next to us. It rumbles under the wall through a low arched tunnel – so low the water almost skims the ceiling. Louder than the river, though, is the sound of *people*. The growl of their engines, the blare of their horns, the bark of their dogs, the shout of their voices, the slam of their doors – nothing I haven't heard before, but not like this. Not all at once. Not apart from on TV anyway. In the forest the sounds of people come slower. One at a time. And not very often.

HONK!

A big blue bus rattles past. *LONDON EXPRESS*. London?

The London?

Jess steers through the shady narrow streets. There

are buildings *everywhere*. Back in the forest there's just the house and the garage and trees and trees and trees and trees. Here, wherever you look there are walls made out of flint or stone or brick. Narrow houses crammed up against other narrow houses and those houses are crammed up against even more. The grey town wall looms up behind everything. You could be forgiven for forgetting there's a forest out there at all, with a little house in the middle of it, with a watchmaker's workshop inside.

And there are so many people. There are people tying strings of green and white flags across the narrow streets – leaning out of windows; wobbling on ladders. There are people shifting tables across roads and unloading boxes out of cars. There are people rushing out of one front door and into another, carrying trays covered with tea towels. The smell of baking curls and flexes under our noses.

"Is it always this busy?" whispers Midge.

"Oh no," says Jess. "This is all for the festival. It's just one day, once a year. But your timing's good, boys – it starts tonight."

"And here we are." Jess turns another tight corner and the ground spreads out into a wide cobbled space. The buildings are all backed up to the edges like none of them wants to be seen showing off in the middle. The clock tower stretches up on the northern side.

Two minutes to ten.

"Is this Sinkly Square?" I say.

"It certainly is," says Jess. She drives past number 105 – Farstoke Framing, 107 – Farstoke Groceries, 109 – Eyes 'n' Ears: Farstoke Optician and Hearing Centre. I've no idea where 106 and 108 and 110 are. We go past 113 and 115, both tiny squeezed-up houses, then pull up outside the next tiny squeezed-up house – 117.

"No place like home, eh?" Jess yanks up the handbrake, turns off the engine and gets out.

"Come on, Midge." I open the door, stick out my leg and put my lifeling foot down for the first time ever on Farstoke ground.

DONG.

I jump half out the seat.

Jess laughs. "Loud, isn't she?"

DONG.

It's the clock tower striking ten.

Jess walks down her front path. It's lined with smiling purple pansies.

DONG.

Yap! Yap-Yap!

Is that a dog?

DONG.

Yap-Yap!

Yes. There. In next door's window. Number 119. Number 119 is not a tiny squeezed-up house. It's two times taller than any of its neighbours. And it's got a quivery little dog inside. A quivery little dog not much good for anything.

DONG.

Yap-Yap!

Midge yanks at my sleeve. "It's that dog again, Lonny," he whispers. "It's Suki."

DONG.

Yap!

"Does that mean those girls live there, too?" he says.

"I don't know, do I? Stop pulling my sleeve."

DONG.

Yap! Yap! Yap!

"Suki!" says Jess. "Be quiet!"

DONG.

Yap! Yap!

"Ignore her, boys." She starts leafing through her enormous bunch of keys. "Bloomin' dog."

DONG.

Yap-yap!

Two hands poke out from under a net curtain, grab Suki round the middle and whisk her away.

"Ah – here it is." Jess singles out a key and unlocks the front door.

DONG.

"Come on in, then." She steps into the house but calls back over her shoulder so we can still hear. "We'll get some tea and then we can talk about work. Are you hungry? Did you have a good breakfast?"

"I, um, no." I push Midge towards the front door.

"We didn't have any breakfa…" My words trail off because there, in Jess's front garden, right next to my foot, is a stone. A flat, round stone propped up for all to see, with a picture carved into it. A picture of a boy sideways on.

And not just any boy. It's a picture of Midge.

"Didn't have any breakfast?" says Jess. "Growing lads like you? We'll have to do something about that, won't we?" She wraps her arm round Midge and draws him into the house. "In there, Midge. First door on the left – that's it, that's the sitting room."

A picture of Midge. On a stone. In the middle of Farstoke.

"Oh – admiring my carving, Lonny?" Jess is back in the doorway again. "Smashing, isn't he? I got him at the festival last year. Why don't you come along tonight? You'd have a lovely time."

What's a picture of Midge doing in a Farstoke front garden? Wearing a long, flowing cloak? I move my head one way and the other. Try looking at it from different angles. Maybe it's not Midge after all. But there's something about it that's exactly like him. The shape of his nose? Or his chin? Or his skinny little arms? Perhaps it's not even a boy, now I look at it closer. Perhaps it's a fairy. Or a pixie.

Whatever it is it's holding something. A flower?

"D'you see that detail on the dandelion?" says Jess. "Amazing. Aren't some people clever?"

A dandelion. Course it is. A seed-head clock, just

like in the field. The boy's cheeks are all puffed up – I see it now. Ready to blow time away.

Jess beams down at the stone. "Farstoke loves a lifeling," she says.

CHAPTER 10

"Are you all right, Lonny? You look quite ill all of a sudden." Jess cups a firm hand on my elbow. "Come on, get yourself inside with your brother. I want you both to think of this as your Farstoke home, where you belong."

Where we belong? I look back at the square. The clock tower is dizzyingly tall. Farstokers bustle and hustle across the hard soil-less ground. There's barely a tree in sight. And right at my feet is a picture of a lifeling.

"Good old destiny," she says. "That's what's brought you here. Destiny. Don't you think?"

"No, no – I… I just wanted…" My mouth has dried

up. I try to gulp it wet.

"Let's get some food down you." Jess guides me into the house. "Skipping breakfast is never a good idea, you know." She closes the front door behind me.

It's OK. It'll be OK. Just get the work done, Lonny, and buy some groceries, and get back to the forest. We don't even need to see many Farstokers. Just Jess. That's all. And maybe the person in the grocery shop.

"Oh – watch out for Waldo," Jess calls down the hall.

Waldo?

Who's Waldo?

She laughs. "Don't look so worried, Lonny. He won't hurt you; he's a big softy – but he'll get under your feet if you don't watch out."

"What's that noise?" whispers Midge.

He twists round and the squidgy, flowery sofa creaks underneath us.

"Stop wriggling, Midge. It's just Jess making tea in the kitchen."

"No. Not that. It's coming from – whoa!"

An enormous rabbit lollops out from behind an armchair, ears flopped down over its cheeks. Midge whips his legs up on to the seat.

"Here you go." Jess comes out of the kitchen with a tray of steaming mugs and piled-up toast. "Breakfast is served – oh, there you are, Waldo. Come to meet our guests?"

The rabbit sniffs at her toes. I swear he's the size of a full-grown badger and I'm not even exaggerating. Just as well it wasn't him I found dying in the forest yesterday. Rabbit that size'd take more than a few days off a lifeling kid.

"Watch out, bunny, or you'll get this whole lot on your head." Jess puts the tray down on a low table. "Help yourself, boys – have as much as you want, there's plenty more. Now, I've been thinking. I've got the perfect jobs for you both. Lonny – David and Daniel from Farstoke Groceries brought their garden furniture round for cleaning last week and it's still sitting there in my back garden. Fancy tackling that after your toast? They'll be ever so pleased to get it done – they're so busy. Between them they pretty much run the whole festival these days, as well as the shop."

"That would be great. Thank you, Jess." I take a slice of honeyed toast from the tray.

"Wonderful. No special training required, just a bit of squirty cleaner and some elbow grease." Jess passes Midge a mug of tea. "And as for you, Midge, the Penhaligons have asked me to sort out all the loose change from their travels. Gave me a whole sackful of cash to separate into different currencies and, believe me, they've been to a lot of places. It's the perfect job for someone with good eyes and small fingers. You can sit at the kitchen table and keep me company while I get on with sewing the sequins on to Tessa

Blakely's latest competition outfit. Sound all right?"

Midge stares at her.

"That sounds perfect," I say. "Doesn't it, Midge?"

"Um, yes," says Midge. "Perfect. Thank you." He takes a sip from his too-hot tea.

Two hours ago I didn't even know there was any such thing as garden furniture. Now I know it inside-out and round-the-bend and backwards: grubby seats, streaked legs, stained tops and dirty underneaths.

I've scrubbed and I've scrubbed and I've brought it all to white again and now it's sitting on Jess's grass looking as shiny as the day it was bought, I reckon.

Jess comes out of the house. "How're you getting on, Lonny?" She shuts the back door firmly behind her. "Got to keep Waldo in. He wouldn't go far but that silly Suki keeps finding her way under the fence."

"Suki?" I say. "The dog from next door?"

"That's the one. Fancies herself as a rabbit hunter. I wouldn't rate her chances against Waldo, though, and I do not want to be the person who has to tell my granddaughters that their dog's been beaten up by a giant rabbit."

"Granddaughters?"

"Oh, yes, my daughter and her family live next door. Two girls, she's got. Erin and Katy. You'll meet them shortly – we'll be going round for lunch."

"Oh no, Mrs, um, Jess. We don't need to go anywhere for lunch. We just want to—"

"Pizza."

"Pardon?"

"I'm doing home-made pizza. Better than the dreadful ones they fill up their freezer with." Jess runs a hand over the top of the shiny garden table. "Oh, these look marvellous, Lonny."

Vvvvvmmmmm

A tingle in my top lip.

No.

No.

Not now.

She tips up a chair and peers underneath. "Couldn't have done a better job myself."

Vvvvvmmmmm

"Er, thank you, Mrs, um, Jess."

Vvvvvmmmmmmmmmm

It's something small and near. On the patio most likely.

Vvvvvmmmmmmmmmmmmmmmm

There. A stag beetle. Curled-up legs. A single flicky wing, stuck out and twisted.

Walk away, Lonny. Just walk away.

"Lonny?" Jess peers at me. "Are you all right?"

Vvvvvmmmmmmmmmmmmmmmmmmmmm

The buzzing creeps along my jaw. I give my head a shake. "Yes. Yes. I'm fine."

Vvvvvmmmmmmmmmmmmmmmmmmmmmmmm

I rub my neck. It's under control. It's only a beetle.

Vvvvvvvmmmmmmmmmmmmmmmmmmmmmmmm

"You look a bit queasy again," says Jess. "I hope I haven't worked you too hard."

"No – it's OK. I'm fine. I just need to get home now really and—"

"Pizza. That's what you need. Midge is round there already – I took him over a few minutes ago. Dropped him off with all the ingredients."

Midge is already there? What on earth does he think he's doing?

Vvvvvvvmmmmmmmmmmmmmmmmmmmmmmm

"I'll just check these, then we'll go and join him." Jess tips a second chair upside down. "Oh, look, you've missed a bit here. No matter, I'll sort it." She picks up the cleaner and squirts the chair.

Vvvvvvvvvvvvvvvmmmmmmmmmmmmmmm

Get rid of it. Got to get rid of it.

"There we go." Jess scrubs the white plastic. "That should—"

STOMP!

I smack my foot down on the beetle. And give it a twist, just to be sure.

Jess stares at the black squidge on the ground.

The buzzing's gone. Just like that.

Jess sets the chair upright. "All living creatures are precious, Lonny."

It's all right. She doesn't know. She *can't* know. No one does.

I swallow. "It was dying."

Jess picks up the squirty cleaner. "Well, we don't

74

know that *for sure*, do we?"

I do. I know it for absolutely, completely sure. I mean, you don't get the buzzing when something's just tired and having a rest, do you? You don't even get it when something's broken a wing and it's sure to die sooner or later as a dead-certain, straight-as-an-arrow consequence. You only get the buzzing when something's properly dying. Right here, right now.

"We must treat all animals with respect, Lonny." Jess looks down the garden and frowns. "Except rats. I have had quite enough of rats munching their way into my shed and I'd be perfectly happy if they all got Pied-Pipered away this very night. Which reminds me, I bought some Rat-Out a couple of days ago and haven't got round to putting it down yet – maybe you could do it after lunch? That should put an end to the pests." She looks back at me and smiles. "But *apart* from rats, all living creatures are precious. Remember that. Now, let's get on. Time to pop next door. All good?"

All good? Not really, no. But I can't exactly turn up home without Midge, can I?

I grab my bag and follow Jess round to number 119.

CHAPTER 11

In the middle of Erin and Katy's hall there's a staircase. It's not a normal staircase like ours at home. It spirals up through the centre of the house. Clockwise, like a honeysuckle stem. We're all gathered round the bottom of it, with Suki yapping at our ankles. Or *my* ankles, more specifically. Midge is hiding behind the banister.

"This is Lonny, Midge's brother," says Jess. "He's helping me out with some work too, just like Midge. Lonny – this is Erin, this is Katy, and this is their dad, Philip – but he's a school teacher so perhaps you should call him Mr Voss."

Everyone laughs, so I laugh too.

"Very nice to meet you, Lonny." Mr Voss is tall and thin and he gives my hand a good firm shake. He's wearing a tie round his neck. It's green with orange spots.

Dad's got some ties in his wardrobe at home. Never seen him wear one, though.

"Lonny and Midge are home-schooled, aren't you, boys?" says Jess. "Their dad teaches them. They live in the forest – did I tell you that?"

"Home-schooled?" Katy, the youngest, is standing on the third stair, swinging on the banister. "You mean – school at home? Can I do that, Dad? I want to be home-schooled like Lonny and Midge."

"Well, you can't," says Erin.

Yap! Yap-yap!

"And this is Suki, of course," says Jess.

Grrrrrrrrrrrrrrrrr.

"Suki!" says Erin. "Stop growling."

"You both have very strange clothes," says Katy.

"Ka-ty!" Erin slaps a hand over her eyes. "You don't have to say everything that comes into your head, you know."

Strange clothes?

"Erin's right, Katy," says Jess. "Please don't make personal comments."

My trousers are a bit short, I s'pose, now I look at them.

And Midge's are a bit long.

And his sleeves come down over his hands.

Erin and Katy's sleeves don't come down over their hands. And their trousers are just the right length.

Suki growls louder. *Grrrrrrrrrrrrrrrr.* She looks me straight in the eye. Not Midge. Not Jess. Just me. I knew coming round here was a bad idea.

"I like Midge's hat, though," says Katy. "It's a nice colour. You're very tall, Lonny. Almost as tall as Dad. How old are you?"

"Ka-ty! Stop!"

"What? What's wrong with that? I'm only asking how old he is. And he *is* tall."

"It's all right," I say. "I'm twelve."

Yap! Yap-yap!

"Twelve?" Mr Voss lifts his eyebrows.

"You look *way* older than that," says Katy.

"Well, I expect the help's quite a blessing for you right now, Jess," says Mr Voss. "You must have a lot of work on, what with the festival and everything."

"The festival!" Katy leaps off the stairs on to the floorboards. "No school! All week!"

"Katy, I've told you not to play on the stairs." Mr Voss flips his tie back and forth through his fingers. Now I look closer they're not spots on it at all. They're fox faces. Tiny orange fox faces with white muzzles and black whiskers.

"You like the tie, Lonny?" he says.

"Mmm?"

"The tie." He holds it out. "Do you like it? It's my favourite. Can you guess why?"

No idea. I shake my head.

"It's our name. *Voss* means 'fox' in German. My wife bought it for me, years ago now." He makes a tired sort of smile.

"Speaking of Alison," says Jess, "how is she today?"

Katy looks up the spiral stairs. Erin scratches the back of her hand. The skin's all red and rough.

"Alison's, um, pretty much the same as she was yesterday." Mr Voss picks at a thread on the end of his foxy tie. "But she got up for a short time this morning, didn't she, girls? Sat on the chair in her bedroom." He rubs his forehead. "She's asleep again now."

"Right," says Jess. "Right. OK." She pulls her face into a smile. "Well, I'd better get on with those pizzas, hadn't I?"

"Oh, Midge." Katy spins round and grabs Midge's hand. "D'you want to see something secret? Come on, I'll show you. It's upstairs."

Midge looks around him like a spooked sparrow.

"Go on," says Jess. "You kids all go and get to know each other. Phil and I will bring the lunch up when it's done. Won't be long – I bought ready-made bases."

"Yay!" calls Katy from the stairs. She's already dragged Midge halfway up to the first floor.

"Here it is." Katy whips something out of an old trunk. The sun shines through a large arched window behind her, swamping the room in light. There's a stripy sofa pushed up against the wall on one side of the room and a tall wooden chest of drawers pushed up against the wall opposite. Two big flowery squashy things sit on the floor in between.

"Ta-daa!" Katy turns round with some kind of green tunic held up in front of her. "Guess who's the lifeling at this year's festival?"

The *lifeling*?

Say nothing, Midge. Say absolutely nothing.

"Ka-ty!" says Erin. "You're not allowed to wear that until Friday."

"No one's going to know." Katy pulls the tunic on over her head. She turns to me and Midge and holds her arms out, like she's done something special.

It's made with hundreds of leaf shapes in lots of different shades of green, all sewn on at their tops. But the bottom bit of each one isn't fixed down, so they're all flapping free.

"It's me!" says Katy. "I'm the lifeling!"

Me and Midge stare at her.

"We had the vote," says Katy.

Me and Midge look at each other.

Katy rolls her eyes. "The vote for who's going to be the lifeling. You do know about the vote, don't you?"

We shake our heads.

"Course they don't." Erin wanders over to the chest of drawers. She opens the top drawer, looks inside and closes it again. "They don't go to our school. They're not from Farstoke, are they?" She opens the next drawer down. "Take that off, Katy, before Gran catches you."

"Well –" Katy kneels down and rummages in the trunk – "at school, every year, just before the festival, we all get to vote for the person who'd make the best lifeling, and then they get to be the lifeling at the festival, see? And this year I won! I've been dying to do it for so long. Last year I came second and I was hoping Artie Daley'd get sick because they'd have to ask me to do it instead but he didn't. And, d'you know what, I'm glad you're not at our school, Midge, because you'd make a *really* good lifeling. You look exactly like one, so you'd definitely get picked. Oh, look! Here's the cape." She pulls out something dark and green and shimmery. "We've got this brilliant costume, see? Because Mum was a lifeling when she was little." She gives the shimmery thing a shake. It ripples out from her fingers.

She stops. "You do know about the festival, don't you?"

"Well," I say, "Jess mentioned something about it earlier but—"

"Erin! They don't even know about the festival!"

"Lucky them." Erin pulls something out of the drawer – a green jumper maybe – and drops it on to the floor by her feet. "It's all totally stupid anyway."

"No it's not!" Katy sweeps the cape behind her and fastens it under her chin. "The festival's the best thing *ever*." She slams down the lid of the trunk and leaps up on top of it. "And the best thing about the festival is the *zip wire*, and the lifeling gets to go first." She grabs the corners of the shimmery cloak and opens out her arms.

Sun from the arched window glows through her wings and paints us all in cool green light.

"Katy Voss!" shouts Katy. "Greatest lifeling ever!" She leaps off the trunk, leaves fluttering, cloak rolling.

Me and Midge scoot backwards.

Thump. She lands in a crumple on the floorboards. The cape floats down on top of her, seconds behind.

"Katy!" says Erin.

"Hey, Midge." Katy springs up, face gleaming. "I've got an idea. Pretend to die!"

What?

Midge looks at me.

"Pretend to die!" says Katy. "Then I can come and save you. Like a real lifeling."

"There's no such thing as a real lifeling, Katy." Erin's on to the fourth drawer now. "Stop hassling our guests." She pulls out a few more clothes – all green – and chucks them on top of the jumper.

"I'm not hassling him. Oh, go on, Midge. Pleeease? Pretend to die!"

"OK," Midge whispers. He closes his eyes and sticks his arms straight down by his sides and tries to stay as still as he can.

He sways side to side. Looks more like someone stood in a light breeze than someone dying.

"That's no good," laughs Katy. "This is how you do it." She grips her throat with one hand, falls on to one of the big flowery squashy things and writhes around on it. "Ahhhhh! Euuurrrgh! Ooooooooofffff!"

"Katy!" says Erin. "Be quiet. Mum's tying to rest. You're making way too much noise."

Katy stops laughing. She gathers up the cape behind her and sits down on the trunk. "You don't say very much, Midge, do you? S'OK, though. I don't mind."

Erin's searching through the bottom drawer.

"OK," says Katy, "I've got another idea. I'm going to tell you the lifeling story."

"*The* lifeling story?" says Erin, yanking out another piece of green clothing.

"Well, all right, *one* of the lifeling stories." Katy's long straight hair has fallen across the cape and now it looks like her hair is shimmering too. She wriggles around a bit on top of the trunk until she's comfy. "This is how it goes." She puts her hands on her lap, closes her eyes and takes a deep breath.

"*It was way back in the days before trains or cars or aeroplanes—*"

This story? This is Grandma Quicke's story.

"*– when everyone went round on, um, wobbly bicycles or snorty horses—*"

My lips start to join in, making the shape of the words. Grandma Quicke's words. I glance at Midge. He's doing the same.

"*– and you had to, um, wind your wristwatch up*

83

every single day or you'd get lost in time. Way back then—"

"Katy, stop," says Erin. 'They're saying the words along with you. They've obviously heard that ridiculous story as many times as we have. They're probably just as sick of it, too." She shuts the bottom drawer, picks up the pile of clothes and dumps it in the middle of the floor.

"*I'm* not sick of it," says Katy. She turns to us. "You do know what a lifeling is, then?"

I nod. "Yeah. We know."

She smiles. "Farstoke loves a lifeling." Then she narrows her eyes. "But do you *believe* in them?"

"Well, I—"

"Of course they don't believe in them," says Erin. "It's only Gran and the other crazy oldies in this town who believe in them."

"*I* believe in them," says Katy.

"But what have lifelings got to do with a festiv—" Midge catches me staring at him and stops mid-sentence.

Shut up. Shut up shut up shut up shut up.

"Lifelings are what the festival's all about! And it's the best thing ever." Katy gets up off the trunk. "There's the Dandelion Offering, and the storytelling, and the Closing of the Gates at midnight. And no one's allowed in or out of Farstoke for a whole twenty-four hours. Like a spell on the town! And there are stories and ceremonies at each gate and the procession in between and best of all there's the zip wire. It's really fun – isn't it, Erin?"

"Well," says Erin, "I s'pose it's fun when you're little. But it's totally stupid really."

"But what's it for?" I say. "What's the point?"

Erin and Katy look at each other. They burst into laughter, and then they both chant together: "*To give thanks and offer gifts, so that one day, when we need one most, a lifeling might appear for us, too.*"

CHAPTER 12

We have to get out.

Out of this room, out of this house, out of Farstoke.

I pull Midge towards the door. "Sorry, we have to go, I've just—"

"Is something wrong?" Katy shimmers in her green cloak.

"No – I just remembered we've—"

"Lunch!" Jess is here, blocking the whole doorway with an enormous tray piled up with pizza. It smells like cheese on toast, but even better.

Katy whips off the cloak and starts yanking the tunic over her head.

Yap! Yap-yap! Suki scurries into the room past

Jess's sparkly boots.

"Katy Voss!" says Jess. "Have you been wearing that outfit before festival day? Take it off. Right now. If bad luck strikes tomorrow, it'll be your—"

"Jess!" Mr Voss appears behind her in the hallway. He's got four stacked-up glasses and a jugful of water. "Please, Jess – don't. Katy, just take it off quickly. You know your gran doesn't want you to wear it before tomorrow."

"Jess," I say, "I'm sorry but Midge and I – we have to go."

"Go?" Jess pushes me back into the room with the tray. "Nonsense. You can't go yet. I won't hear of it. For a start I haven't paid you for this morning's work. And you're going to put that rat poison down for me this afternoon. And I just made industrial amounts of pizza so you have to help us eat it. Here, Midge, take a plate and a slice; go on, that's it. Good. Lonny, you too, that's it. Perfect."

Jess loads our plates up with stretchy, tomatoey pizza.

"Listen, girls." Mr Voss puts the water down on top of the chest of drawers. "I'm going up to the Northgate to help with the floodlights for tonight's ceremony."

"And I'm popping along for bit too," says Jess. "So, Erin and Lonny, you're in charge. I won't be long. Back by two thirty. And don't worry, boys – I haven't forgotten about Farstoke Groceries. I'll take

87

you there later, OK?"

"And please, girls," says Mr Voss, "remember to be quiet for your mother."

I've never had pizza before.

Pizza is probably the most delicious thing I've ever tasted in my life.

Pizza is almost delicious enough to make you forget you're a lifeling sitting here in a house full of Farstokers. Almost, but not quite.

"Are those festival clothes you got out, Erin?" Katy nods at the green heap in the middle of the floor. She's squeezed up with Midge on one of the flowery squashy things. I'm on the other one. Beanbags, she calls them. Midge is sitting rigid and upright but Katy's all arms and legs all over the place.

"Mmmmm," says Erin with her mouth full. She's got the sofa to herself with Suki. She's leaning a bit to one side, legs tucked up underneath her. She looks like a painting. Not an old-fashioned painting where the girls have fans and ringlets and flouncy dresses. A new sort, where they have pizza and stripy T-shirts and messy brown hair.

"Did you find anything for Dad?" says Katy.

"Mmmmmm," says Erin.

Midge tries to bite the stretchy, stringy cheese while also keeping his elbows tucked tight into his sides. It's not working.

"And did you find anything for Mum?" says Katy.

Erin gulps down her mouthful. "Mum won't be coming."

Katy wipes her greasy chin with the back of her hand. "She might still want to wear something festivally, though, mightn't she? And we can open her window. She'll *hear* the festival, even if she can't go."

"Is your mum sick?" The words come out of my mouth without me even thinking.

Erin glares at me. "None of your business."

"Erin!" says Katy. "Who's being rude *now*? He only asked a question." She shifts round on the beanbag. "Yes, she's sick, but they don't know what it is, and because they don't know what it is they can't make her better."

Erin puts her pizza back down on her plate.

"And," says Katy, "she's getting worse. Dad and Gran and Erin keep telling me *don't worry, Katy, everything's going to be fine*, but they're lying."

Erin stares at the floor.

"I know they're lying," says Katy, "because otherwise why's Gran here so often? She never usually comes every day. And Dad keeps whispering with the nurses. And Erin keeps whispering with Dad. They think I can't hear. But they're wrong. I heard them talking about Mum going to a hospice, so she must be really ill because a hospice is where people go to die."

Midge looks at me.

Say nothing, Midge. Nothing.

"That's not true," says Erin. "People go to hospices

for all kinds of reasons. Sometimes they just go for a break. So that's just not true."

Katy pushes what's left of her pizza around her plate. "The rest is, though, isn't it? Mum *is* getting worse."

Erin sucks her cheeks in. "I'm going to check on her." She gets up and sticks her plate down on the sofa.

Katy jumps up, making Midge sink down further into the beanbag. "I'm coming too."

Suki slurps her tongue over the edge of Erin's plate.

"Suki!" Erin whips it away. "No, Katy, I'm going by myself and—"

"But—"

"And if she's up to it, *then* you can go and see her. Gran left me in charge, remember?"

Katy slumps back down. "All right," she says.

Erin puts her plate on top of the chest of drawers and goes out of the room.

Katy leans forward and fishes something green off the clothes pile. She holds it up. It's the jumper Erin got out first. It's knitted and huge, with long droopy arms. Katy pulls a face and drops it back down.

Midge stares at me. I know what he's thinking.

Same as what I'm thinking. *We have to get out.*

Katy pushes the stuff around in the pile.

Forget Jess's rats. That's what he's thinking. *Forget the money. Forget the groceries.*

Katy picks up a green jacket. She wrinkles her nose, drops it down and picks out a third green thing.

We have to get –

Hold on. The third green thing is a T-shirt.

It's got one word on the front, in white capital letters.

LIFE.

CHAPTER 13

I almost choke on my pizza. "Where did you –"

Suki pricks up her ears.

Katy lowers the T-shirt and peeps over the top at me.

"How did you –" I swallow. "Where did you get that?"

"Where did we get it?"

"Yes. It's not yours. It belongs to my – I mean, I've seen it before. It belongs to someone else."

I stick my plate on the floor and jump up.

Grrrrrrrrrrrrrrrr.

I grab the T-shirt.

It's not Katy's. It's my mother's.

I scrunch it up. Hold it to my face.

Katy laughs. "It *is* ours. Look – it's got a name label." She finds the collar and turns it inside out and there it is – a stubby little sewn-on tag. *Voss.*

But anyone can sew a label on to anything, can't they?

"And look –" she waves her hand at the heap of clothes – "there are *loads* of them. They make them for the festival. *Everyone's* got one." She dips into the pile again and pulls out another smaller identical T-shirt.

LIFE.

"And another." She pulls out a third one.

LIFE.

And a fourth.

"Hold on," says Midge. "That one's not the same – it doesn't say 'life'. It says 'ling'."

He's right.

LING.

Katy laughs again. "It *is* the same, silly. They're all like that." She twists T-shirt number four round. "*LIFE* on the front, and *LING* on the back. Lifeling, see? *LIFE. LING.*" She twists it from front to back and back to front. Suki bounds off the sofa and jumps up at the swishing shirt.

Yap-yap!

I hold up T-shirt number one. I twist it round.

LIFE.

LING.

"There must be a million of these in Farstoke," says Katy. "Course you've seen one before. *Everyone's* seen one."

LIFE.

LING.

Erin comes back into the room. "Mum wants to see us." She glances at me. "All of us. Lonny and Midge too. She says she's really glad there's someone else round. Says it's ages since she had proper visitors."

"Hurray!" Katy dumps the T-shirts back on to the pile but I've still got hold of the first one. I turn it frontways, backways, frontways, backways. Did my mother go to a lifeling festival?

Katy takes the T-shirt from me and chucks it on top of the pile.

"But I need to find out where these are sold," I say. "I need to speak to the person who—"

"Come on! Let's go and see Mum." Katy grabs Midge's hand and pulls him up. "Lonny, you can get as many T-shirts as you want at the festival tomorrow." She stops. "You are coming to the festival, aren't you?"

"No," I say. "So if you could just tell me where I can—"

"But you have to," says Katy. "You can go on the zip wire and everything."

"Katy, they don't have to do anything," says Erin. "He just said they're not coming. And anyway, you can't go asking any old people to the festival. It's for

Farstokers."

"They're not any old people! They already know the stories! They practically *are* Farstokers!"

"Katy, just stop! You need to be calmer than this if you're going to be around Mum. Come on – we'd better go now, while she's still awake."

"Lonny?" Midge grabs my arm as I head into the hallway. "Lonny," he whispers. "We should go home. We should go straight home, right now."

Fretty blinkin' Midge. I twist my arm out of his grip and follow Erin and Katy across the landing.

Erin opens the door and whispers through the gap. "We're here, Mum."

Suki scampers in past our ankles.

The room is big. It's wide and light and clean. A fine creamy see-through curtain ripples in front of the open window. Floorboards creak softly under our feet.

But even though it's light and clean and creamy there's something about it that reminds me of Grandad's room.

A stuffiness, maybe. A someone's-been-in-here-too-longness.

Suki patters around. Her claws tap-tap-tap on the wooden boards.

Erin goes over to the bed.

I think it's empty at first. Mrs Voss is a small hump under the fresh white duvet. She's a pool of lank hair on the pillow. She's the almost invisible fall and rise of a chest beneath the covers.

"Here you go, Mum." Erin rearranges the pillows and helps her sit more upright.

"This is our mum." Katy climbs up on to the bed. She lies down with her head on her mother's lap. "Her name's Alison."

Mrs Voss smiles. Dark, yellow dips hollow her cheeks.

Midge tucks himself behind me.

"Hello, Mrs Voss. I'm Lonny and this is Midge. Very pleased to meet you." I hold out my hand. A boot-stuffing, life-giving hand.

"Lonny," hisses Midge. "Don't!"

I ignore him. There's no hint of a buzzing. She's not dying. Not right now anyway.

"Hello, Lonny. Hello, Midge." Her hand is so light, so thin, it's almost not there at all. Her wrists and elbows are awkward and bony. And her voice is a whisper, like Midge's. "Call me Alison," she says. "Gosh, you're a big lad, aren't you?"

"He's only twelve," says Katy. "But he looks way older, doesn't he?"

"He certainly does." Mrs Voss – *Alison* – strokes Katy's head. Soft. Warm. "Where are you from, boys? Are you new to Farstoke?"

"We live in the forest," I say. "A few miles north. Not far. Jess brought us here in Celia."

"How wonderful. It's so long since I've been to

the forest. It's so long since I've even been out of this house. What's it like out there? Are the bluebells in bloom?"

"They're not as good as they were a couple of weeks ago," I say.

"I know how they feel." Alison smiles. It makes her look younger. And not so sick. "I'm not always like this, you know. I had energy once. And the strength to get out and do things. Remember how I used to shout up those stairs, girls?"

"You'll shout up them again," says Erin. "When you're better."

Katy blinks. Rubs her eyes with her sleeve.

"Lonny?" says Alison.

"Yes?"

"I wonder if you'd do something for me?"

Do something?

"Lonny," whispers Midge. "We should go." Tug, tug, tug.

"Well…" I shove Midge away. "I … um…"

Erin pushes Alison's hair from her eyes.

"I suppose it depends on what it is you want done, Mrs, er, Alison," I say.

Her breathing is wheezy. Troubled. "You're a big lad," she says. "Would you help me to go outside? There's somewhere I want to visit. I can't ask the girls – they're not strong enough to support me – but you are, Lonny."

"Mum," says Erin, "you can't go outside. What

would Dad and Gran say?"

Alison swallows. She licks her dry lips. "Dad and Gran make too much fuss. I know they're doing what they think is best for me." She reaches for Erin's hand, presses it softly to her lips. Kisses. Kind words. "But I need to go out. Breathe the air. See the town, and the sky. Feel a little cold on my face. Listen to the birds and the buses and the barking dogs and whatever else is going on out there. I need to visit somewhere I've been happy."

The edges of memories.

"You've been happy here, though, haven't you?" says Katy. "At home?"

"Of course," says Alison, "but I've been stuck here so long now; it all just reminds me of being ill." She smiles at me again. Her face rounds, her eyes brighten. "Will you help me, Lonny? I just want to go round the corner, to the little bridge."

Katy sits up. "Where we used to play Poohsticks? Oh, say yes, Lonny, say yes! Dad and Gran'll be ages yet – we've got plenty of time, haven't we, Erin? It's not far."

Erin sighs. She pulls her mobile phone out of her pocket. "We've got an hour. I'm not sure about this, though. Are you really feeling up to it, Mum?"

"Completely," whispers Alison.

"Oh, go on, Lonny," says Katy. "Say you'll do it."

"Please, Lonny," says Alison. "Just for a short time."

A blur of hair. A turning head.

I look to Erin. She bites her lips between her teeth.

No, no, no, mouths Midge.

Fretty blinkin' Midge.

Erin gives me a nod.

"OK," I say. "I'll help."

"Yay!" says Katy.

Yap! Yap-yap!

Erin picks Suki up off the floor. "I'm afraid you're going to have to stay at home, Sukes. If we're looking after Mum we don't need to be worrying about you as well." And she kisses the little dog right in the middle of her skinny wet nose.

CHAPTER 14

I take pretty much all of Alison's weight as we make our slow way out of the house, down the front path and into Sinkly Square. Not that she's heavy. I reckon she weighs about as little as anyone can weigh and still be alive, but it's still hard work when you're almost carrying a whole person.

I can feel her fragile bones under my hands. Like picking up Layla.

She grips on to me, tight as she can. We're fixed firm.

"Thank you," she says, so only I can hear. "Thank you, Lonny."

"What are those people doing?" whispers Midge.

He points at two men trying to get a tall pole to stay upright in the middle of the square. The pole's got a thick snake of green ribbons falling from the top, coiling on the ground below.

"They're hanging the canopy for the festival," says Erin.

"I love it when the canopy goes up," says Katy.

A little gust of wind whips across the cobblestones. The ribbon-snake ripples.

We head along the edge of the square and turn off into a narrow street, and there's that big blue bus again, stood at a bus stop. *LONDON EXPRESS*, it says on the side. *Every two hours, every day of the week.*

"Hey, Midge, guess what?" says Katy. "I went on that bus once. Didn't I, Mum? We went together. All four of us. It took *ages*. Didn't it, Mum?"

"It did," says Alison.

The street turns into a bridge. There are houses all along it on the left-hand side. It's only when you look to your right you see there's water underneath, and a whole river stretching away, with horse chestnuts stood in a row beside it. And there, not so far away at all, is a second bridge.

"There it is," shouts Katy. "Poohsticks Bridge! I saw it first!"

It's a footbridge. Made of the same stone and flint as most of the houses.

"Come on, Midge. Come with me!" Katy starts

scooping up twigs and branches from under the trees.

"You warm enough, Mum?" says Erin. "It's colder than I thought it'd be."

"I'm fine. I just need to sit down for while."

She doesn't look very fine. She's hunched over. Her whole body heaves with every breath. I help her on to a bench. Erin makes sure her jacket's zipped right up to her chin.

"Erin, you're fussing," says Alison. "You're as bad as your dad." But she's got a smile on her face again. She leans back and closes her eyes, like she's trying to feel and taste and hear and smell the outside without the whole business of seeing getting in the way.

The river gurgles and froths. Seems even faster here than up at the dandelion field. Deeper too, I reckon.

"Come on, Midge, get some sticks." Katy's got a whole armful now, but Midge is standing way back from the river, staring at the water like it's going to leap out and bite him.

"Is he all right?" says Erin.

"He'll be OK," I say.

"Go on, you two." Alison nods towards Katy. "Go and help. I'd like to sit here for a bit on my own. Play Poohsticks like you used to, Erin. I'd like to watch."

I shove my hands in my pockets and follow Erin over to the trees. Katy's gathered up so many sticks she can hardly hold them all.

"That's got to be enough, hasn't it?" says Erin. "How long are you expecting to—"

"It's Rin!" Two girls, about the same age as Erin, wave at us from the other side of the river.

"Rinny! Rinny! Hiya, Rinny!"

Rinny?

Erin waves back. "Hi, Yaz. Hi, Flissie."

Oh. *Rin*, as in E-*rin*.

"Hold on, we're coming across." The girls giggle over the bridge. They pause a moment to stare at Alison. Alison waves.

"Who's that lady?" says Yaz or Flissie.

"That's our mum," says Katy.

"Your *mum*?" says Flissie or Yaz. "That's never your mum. Your mum looks totally different from that."

"She's ill," says Erin.

"Again? I thought she was ill last year?"

"Well, she never really got better."

"Oh. Poor thing," says Yaz or Flissie. "She looks *terrible.*"

They both stare up at me. "Well," says Flissie or Yaz, "aren't you going to introduce us, Rin?"

"Oh," says Erin. "Yes. Sorry. This is Lonny, and that's his brother Midge over there."

"Pleased to, um, meet you." Should I hold my arm out, for handshaking? Yaz and Flissie don't seem to want it. Their eyes travel all the way down to my feet then back up to my head. They give each other a look.

Erin scratches the back of her hand. "They're not really our *friends*," she gabbles out. "They're just doing some work for—"

"Of course they're our friends!" says Katy.

"Well, yes," says Erin. "What I mean is—"

"What's the little one doing all the way over there?" says Flissie or Yaz.

"He just doesn't like the water," I say. "That's all."

"Riiiight," says Yaz or Flissie. "Well, we'd better get going. We're helping to set up the square for the festival."

"Yeah." Flissie or Yaz rolls her eyes. "The stupid festival."

The other one laughs. "Yes – the *Stupid* Festival. They should rename it that."

"Still," says Flissie or Yaz, "at least we get the week off school. See you at the Stupid Festival tomorrow, Rin? We can hang out together."

"Um, yeah," says Erin. "That'd be great. See you tomorrow."

"OK! Bye, then! Bye! Bye!" Yaz and Flissie drift away towards Sinkly Square, calling back over their shoulders.

"Hope your mum gets better soon!"

"Yeah – hope she gets better soon! Bye! Bye!"

"Bye," says Erin. She waves at their backs.

"Phew," says Katy. "Glad *they* didn't hang around long. Come on, Midge. Let's go up on the bridge. Come on!" She marches off with her millions of sticks.

Erin sighs. She stoops down, picks up a twig.

She bends it backwards and forwards, forwards and

backwards. It snaps.

"There's a trick, y'know," I say.

She looks up. "A trick?"

"To winning Poohsticks."

She blinks back the tears in her eyes. "What is it, then?"

"You've just got to choose the right stick." I spot a good one a few steps away. "Like this." I pick it up. "It's thick, see? And smooth. No greenery. Won't get caught up in the weeds." I pick up a couple more and pass them all to Erin. "Here, have these. Don't tell Midge, though."

She smiles. "Or Katy."

There are two stone steps right in the middle of the bridge, one on either side, against each wall. Katy's standing on the upstream one, leaning over and waving to her mum below.

"Katy!" says Erin. "Get down."

"It's OK to stand on this. Mum always used to let me."

"Ages ago! You're tall enough to see without it now. Stop leaning! Last thing we need is you toppling off the bridge. It's a long way down, y'know."

"You're not my mother! Stop bossing me around. Come on. Let's do Poohsticks." She waves a thin leafy twig in Erin's face. "Ready?"

Midge is standing right in the middle of the bridge, as far away from either side as possible. He's clutching a twig as leafy as Katy's.

"Look, you're going to have to let Midge stand on the steps," says Erin. "See? He's not as tall as you. He won't even be able to chuck his stick in otherwise."

Katy grumbles and we all shove a protesting Midge up on to the step. He's quivering like Suki.

"Ready, then?" says Katy. "On three. One! Two! THREE!"

We hurl our sticks down into the river and me and Erin and Katy rush to the other side.

"Come on, Midge." Katy goes back, grabs Midge and drags him across.

"There!" I shout. "It's mine. It's definitely mine."

"And that's mine!" says Erin.

"Aw," says Katy, still peering over the edge. "I bet mine's got stuck."

"Lonny always wins Poohsticks," whispers Midge.

"Let's have another go," says Katy.

We play again. And again. And again. By the fifth time Midge is running to the edge like everyone else without needing to be dragged. It's always me or Erin who wins, though.

"OK," says Katy. "That's it. I'm fed up of playing with you two. It's just me against Midge now, all right?"

"All right, all right. Go ahead," says Erin.

They race off to grab more sticks.

Erin looks out towards the bank. She waves at Alison. "It's nice of you to help Mum like this."

I lean on the side of the bridge, elbows pressing into sharp flint. Mayflies bob and swoop above the water.

"My mum died," I say.

Erin scratches the back of her hand.

Stupid thing to say, Lonny. Stupid, stupid thing to say. "I'm sorry, I mean, that's nothing to do with your mum, I shouldn't have—"

"It's all right," she says.

Katy and Midge run across the bridge and peer over the side.

"There!" It's Midge. Laughing. Smiling. Shouting, even. "It's mine! I won! I won!"

"Aw," says Katy, but she's laughing too. "Come on!"

They run back again, grabbing more sticks on the way.

"Was she ill?" says Erin. "Your mum?"

I shake my head. "No. She was fine. She went into hospital to have Midge, but it all went wrong. She didn't come out again."

"One, two, three! Quick! Quick!" Katy dodges across the bridge and Midge chases after her, clutching his stomach from laughing so much. Never seen him like that. Never seen him anything even close to like that.

"Do you miss her?" says Erin.

I nod. I miss her all the time.

Erin waves a mayfly away from her face.

"They only live for a day," I say.

"Who do?"

"Mayflies. Just twenty-four hours. Well, that's not *exactly* true. They can spend months as larvae in the river, hoping not to get eaten by a trout. They don't even know there's anything else in the universe except their underwater world. Then one day they grow wings and they fly up out of the water. And after that they've got one day before they die. Twenty-four hours."

Erin swishes another one away from her face. "D'you think one day feels like a hundred years, though, to a mayfly?"

"Dunno." I watch the insects dance and dive. "Maybe. They look like they're enjoying it anyway, don't they?"

Erin leans her elbows on the bridge, just like me. Blows a cooling breath on the back of her hands.

"Erin?" I say. "Those T-shirts, the ones Katy had, with the words on. She said you can buy them at your festival. D'you know where I can find the people who sell them?"

"The lifeling T-shirts?"

"Yes. My mum had one. I've seen it in photographs. And I thought if I could find the person who sold it to her, maybe they'd…"

It sounds stupid now I'm saying it out loud. There's a million of those T-shirts in Farstoke. Everyone's got one, just like Katy said. Who's going to remember someone buying one over twelve years ago?

"Maybe they'd remember?" Erin gazes out across the water. "And maybe they'd be able to tell you about her?"

"Well, yeah. Does that sound stupid?"

"No," she says. "It doesn't sound stupid at all."

DONG.

The clock tower.

"Two o'clock," shouts Katy.

DONG.

"Only ten hours till they close the gates!" She jumps up and down in the middle of the bridge.

The Closing of the Gates.

"Do they really not let anyone in or out for the whole festival?" I ask.

"Crazy, isn't it? Come on, Gran'll be finished soon. We'd better start getting Mum back home."

CHAPTER 15

I can see why a rat might like it in Jess's shed. It's only a draughty glue-and-plank eight-footer but it's jam-packed full of gardening tools and bags of soil and packets of seed and old potatoes and threaded garlic and sacks of hay and rabbit food. I clear a corner free and put down the Rat-Out, just like it says on the packet. Then I tuck the half-empty box under my arm and make triply sure I'm leaving the door shut good and tight behind me. Doesn't matter how deadly Rat-Out is, it won't be much use if the hedgehogs get at it first.

Yap! Yap-yap!

Suki. Look at her. She's here again – sniffing at Jess's

back door. Looking for Waldo.

She spots me. *Grrrrrrrrrr.*

She whips her wispy, quivery self round and darts over, lips drawn back, sharp teeth bared.

Yap! Yap!

I stumble into the flower beds, dropping the box. Rat poison scatters all over the place.

For heaven's sake, Lonny. She's only tiny. You're as bad as Midge. And she stopped a metre away from me anyway. *All talk and no gumption*, Grandad'd say.

Grrrrrrrrrr.

"Oh, go away, Suki." I pick myself up and try to scoop the Rat-Out back into the box. "Look what you made me do."

Grrrrrrrrrrr.

Suki edges round me and sniffs at the pellets.

"Oh no, no, no," I say. "You can't eat that." I grab her round her skinny middle and carry her squirming and growling back to number 119.

Erin opens the door. "Suki – how on earth did you get out again?"

The little dog can't get away from me fast enough. She scrabbles out of my arms and hurls herself into Erin's.

"Thanks for bringing her back, Lonny." Erin twists her head away from Suki's slurping tongue. "And … thanks for today too. It was really kind, what you did for Mum."

"Oh. That's all right. It was, um, fun. I mean, no,

sorry, I don't mean…"

"It's OK – it *was* fun." Erin smiles, so I smile back.

"Is she OK?" I say. "Your mum?"

"Yes. She's sleeping now."

"OK. That's good." My trousers are covered in dirt from Jess's flower beds. I try to brush it off. "We're … um … going to Farstoke Groceries now, and after that Jess is driving us home."

"Lonny," says Erin, "that thing I said earlier – about the festival being just for Farstokers – I'm sorry. I didn't mean it. Actually it'd be really good if you and Midge came. We could show you round and stuff. I mean, I'm just offering. In case you change your mind."

I shake my head. "Thanks, but I won't be changing my mind. But the T-shirts, the lifeling ones, do you know who sells them?"

"Oh, the T-shirts. Yes. Sorry – I don't really know anything about them."

"Right. OK. Never mind." It doesn't matter. It was a ridiculous idea in the first place. No one's really going to remember my mother. And I don't even have any time left anyway. I've got to get the shopping –

"But I can find out," says Erin. "Tomorrow – at the festival. And then we can go and visit them next time you're here. How about that?"

Next time I'm here? Well, yes. I suppose I could come back.

Farstoke's really not as bad as Dad and Grandad

have made out all these years. I mean, Jess probably puts that lifeling stone away as soon as the festival's done, doesn't she? And Katy probably puts her shimmering cloak back into that trunk. And no one probably even thinks about lifelings again until next year.

"Well, yeah, that'd be great. That'd be really great. Thanks, Erin."

She smiles. One side of her mouth lifts up a little bit higher than the other. She looks like a painting all over again.

DONG.

The clock tower.

DONG.

DONG.

Only nine hours until they close the gates.

Celia rumbles through the forest, Country Hits blasting out of the radio.

"Why, why, why dontcha come a-knockin'? Dontcha come a knockin' on my door no more!" sings Jess.

I hold my rucksack on my lap. It's crammed to the brim with all the things I bought in Farstoke Groceries. The sky's turning dark.

"Why, why, why dontcha come a-askin'? Dontcha come a-askin' for my kisses no more!"

"It's going to rain," says Midge.

"Rain?" Jess laughs. "It won't rain. It never rains in festival week."

"Not ever?" says Midge.

"Never. It can't – it'd ruin the dandelions."

I lean forward and look up to the treetops. It's clearly going to chuck it down any minute. Maybe Erin's right. Maybe Jess is a crazy oldie.

"Another pear drop?" Jess shakes the bag under our noses, keeping her eyes on the road. "Now, boys," she says, "I know you don't want to come to the festival, but you'll come back to Farstoke afterwards, won't you? I'm sure I can find you a few more jobs to do. The money you earned today won't last forever, will it? More's the pity."

She's right. The money won't last forever. So I'm going to have to come back anyway. So I might as well see Erin at the same time, mightn't I? And we might as well go and look for whoever sold Mum her T-shirt.

"Yes," I say. "That'd be great. Thanks, Jess."

"And you too, Midge," says Jess. "You and your back-to-front hat. You'll come back after the festival as well, won't you?"

Midge crunches his pear drop. "Could I see Katy again?" he says.

"Katy? Of course you can. Oh, look. We're nearly at your house." She steers Celia through the sparsening trees, turns off the road and rolls on to our gravel.

"Hey, look – Dad's up, Lonny," says Midge. "He's out of bed."

He's right. There's Dad in the kitchen window.

"Oh, that's nice." Jess pulls up the handbrake. "I

114

expect he'll be pleased to see—"

"Get out!" The front door flies open and Dad leaps across the driveway. "Get out!" He almost yanks the passenger door off its hinges. "You two – out of that van. Now!"

He shoves us towards the house and roars at Jess. "Where have you been with my boys?"

CHAPTER 16

"Dad! Stop! Jess just gave us some—"

"Get in the house, Lon!" Dad leans in towards Jess, hands clamped to the edge of Celia's roof and head slung Big-Bad-Wolf-like between his shoulders. "I want to know where you've been with my boys, and what the hell you've been doing."

"I, um, I'm sorry, Mr Quicke." Jess's voice shakes. "I didn't mean any—"

"I don't care what you *meant*; I want to know what you've been doing."

"Dad! Stop!" says Midge. "She didn't do anything!"

"Get in the house."

"Mr Quicke," says Jess, "Lonny and Midge wanted

some work. You should be very proud of them."

"Did you take my boys to Farstoke?" Dad's voice has gone quiet.

Not a good sort of quiet, though. A holding-it-back-and-strapping-it-down-because-it's-too-dangerous-to-let-loose sort of quiet.

"They said you were OK wi—"

"Did you take my boys to Farstoke?"

"Well, I—"

"Leave her alone, Dad."

"Lonny, I told you to get in the house."

"But Jess hasn't done anything wrong. I asked her to give me some work, so I could earn some money. There was no food. Jess helped us. She gave us jobs."

"Jobs? What jobs?"

"Look." I open my rucksack. "We bought food. Bread, milk, tea. So we can all eat."

Dad picks out a slab of cheese. Drops it back in. He rubs his eyes. You'd never think he'd been in bed for ages. Thought you were supposed to look better after a long sleep, not worse.

He leans into the van again. "Go away, Jess," he growls. "And *stay* away."

Her hands are shaking on the wheel. "Will you be OK, Lonny? You and Midge?"

"We'll be fine, Jess. Thank you for everyth—"

Clunk! Dad slams Celia's door shut. "Get in the house."

Midge's eyes brim with tears.

"Inside! Both of you! Now!"

The wheels grind and twist in the gravel as Jess turns Celia round and drives back into the forest.

"Give me that." Dad snatches my rucksack. He takes out the cheese and slams it on to the kitchen table.

Midge stares at it.

"Dad, I—"

"I can't believe you did this." He pulls out eggs. *Slam!* Milk. *Slam!* Biscuits. *Slam!* "After all I taught you. After everything I've done. I promised your mother I'd keep you safe – and you go and take yourself off to Farstoke! Why would you do that to me? Why would you put yourself at risk like that? Why would you do it to your grandad? He's been worried sick." He chucks my rucksack on to the floor.

"But you were in bed!" I pick up the bag. "There was nothing to eat. And look – look at all the food I got."

"Doesn't matter what you got."

Doesn't matter?

"Go upstairs," he says. "Go upstairs, tell your grandad you're safe, and then … then just stay up there. I don't even want you coming down. And, Midge – get into the workshop. We're making those watches again, from scratch."

Doesn't matter?

I've *saved* us. I've *fed* us. I've stopped us from starving.

What are we going to eat tonight? Pocket watches?

No. We're going to eat the food that *I* bought. With the money that *I* earned. That's what.

STOMP-STOMP-STOMP-STOMP-STOMP.

I crash up the stairs and Grandad's already waiting with his bedroom door open wide.

"Than kevans than kevans than kevans." He grabs me with his papery, wobbly hands. "What about the tiddler? Is he here? Is he safe?"

"Midge is fine, Grandad. There's no need to worry."

His eyes are swimming in old-man tears and his hair's sticking up even more than normal. "I knew she'd trundled you off to Farstoke – I knew she had. Thought you weren't never coming home."

"It's OK, Grandad. I'm OK. We both are."

"You shouldn't have gone, Lonny. We might never have gottled you back again."

"Look, I'm fine. It was all right there – they were nice to us. It's not as bad as you think it is."

"It might've seemed good and dandy in Farstoke this one time," he says. "It might even seem good and dandy two times, or three times, or four. But the more good and dandy it seems, Lonny, the more worse it is. Are you listening to me? Are you coggling? The gooder and dandier it acts, the more dangerouser it is."

Night-time hovers at the window.

I'm still here. Back in the forest. Curled up on my

bed. *Safe.*

I reach up. Touch the map. Feel the edge of the world.

London. Paris. Prague.

I drop my arm down again.

Haven't been out to see Layla. Haven't had anything to eat. Didn't even get up when Grandad started shouting for teatime.

Midge's bed is empty.

My stomach rumbles.

Get up, Lonny. Get up and find some food.

It's *your* bread down there after all. *Your* cheese. *Your* milk. *Your* eggs. *Your* tea.

I heave myself up off the bed and trudge downstairs.

There's no one in the kitchen.

"Lonny? S'that you?"

Midge is on his own in the workshop. The favourite son, with his clever little hands and his clever little working specs and his clever little anglepoise lamp. He never got sent upstairs, did he?

"Course it's me."

He flips up the specs. He blinks. "Dad shouldn't have shouted at Jess, should he?"

I pick at the peeling paint on the door frame.

"I like Jess," he says. "And Katy. And Erin."

A big flake of paint comes right off the wood.

"D'you think we really will go back to Farstoke one day?" he says.

There's a smell. Reminds me of autumn. Cold

nights. Damp leaves. Sharp apples.

It's smoke. I crinkle my nose. "I can smell burning, Midge. What's burning?"

"Oh, that's Dad. He's having a bonfire."

Bonfire. Course it is.

I leave Midge to his tweezers and springs and head for the back door. Pull on my boots.

Better go and see Dad. He must've calmed down now if he's having a bonfire.

And he was only trying to look after me, I s'pose. Doing what he thinks is best. Doesn't even realise he's been completely wrong. For years and years and years.

There he is. Down the bottom, almost at the trees. The fire cage is stacked full, popping and crackling and burning bright. A heady mix of flames and ash and forest air sweeps through my brain, clears my mind. Makes me feel wide awake.

Dad's standing right up close. Fists in his pockets, shoulders hunched. Staring at the twisting smoke. His face flickers orange.

Vvvvvd.

Vvvvvvd.

Tiny creatures dart to their deaths in the flames. No time to save them. They barely even give me a tingle.

Vvvd.

I can't stand as close to the fire as Dad. It burns at my cheeks.

"All right?" I say.

"Mmmmm?" He stares at the flames like I'm not even here.

"You all right? You stayed in bed all day yesterday."

"Oh. Yes. Yes. I'm fine. No problem." He picks up a stick. Pokes through the bars of the cage. Shifts something further into the fire.

"I'm, uh, I'm sorry about earlier," he says. "It wasn't Jess's fault. I know that."

What is that he's burning? It's not just garden stuff. There's something soft in there too. Material. Clothes?

"You don't need to worry, Dad. About me going to Farstoke. I can look after myself. Really. If I get the buzzing, I can walk away and—"

"It's not your fault, either, Lon." He gives the fire another poke. "It's not anyone's fault except mine."

What's that – in the middle of the cage? Is that a book or something? What's he burning books for?

"I promised your mother I'd look after you," he says. "They were my very last words to her. I promised I'd keep you right here, in the forest, where you're safe. I've let her down. I've let you both down."

"No, you haven't. You haven't let anyone down. I *am* safe. You've taught me how to walk away and—"

"I should've done this years ago. Instead I kept it all – photographs, clothes – and you found them, Lonny, and it made you want to leave the forest. I understand that, I really do. I'm not blaming you. It's all my fault."

The photos?

"But it's OK, Lon. Don't worry. I'm dealing with it now. It's under control. I'll get rid of it – all her stuff. All those things that made you want to leave. And then everything will be all right."

I step closer to the fire.

Burning cheeks, burning nose, burning eyes. I don't even care.

It's not a book. It's Mum's album. Right there in the middle.

CHAPTER 17

I snatch the stick from Dad.

"Lonny!"

I stab at the cage. Can I push the album out? Wedge it away from the flames?

I run round the other side, try pushing it back the other way.

"Lonny, leave it." Dad chases after me. "You've got to let it go."

I shove him away.

I poke and stab at the fire. Mum's clothes are in there, too. Brown knitted gloves. Black woolly hat. Shrivelled and burnt and melted.

Poke! Stab! Poke! Stab!

"Lonny, let it burn. Say goodbye. She's not coming back, see? She's never coming back."

The album isn't moving.

Got to put the fire out. Got to put it out right now.

I race up to the shed for the hose, drag it to the house and jam it on to the outside tap.

I run back down the garden with the other end of it. Point the nozzle at the bonfire – but the water stops. A kink in the hose somewhere. I run back and straighten it. Try again. It dribbles out. Another blinkin' kink. I snake the end of the hose to try and straighten it out.

All it gives me is drip drip drip drip drip.

I collapse on to the grass, clutching the end of the hose. The dribbling end of the stupid, blinkin' hose.

Tears brim up behind my eyes.

Flames loom above the cage.

Smoke tumbles into the sky.

Too late.

Too blinkin' late.

Specks of ash flutter down. The last tiny glimpses of my mother.

I take the stairs four at a time.

I tear my map off the bedroom wall, fold it up and stuff it into my bag. Grab my jacket and a torch.

Then I run down – oof! Straight into Midge.

I knock him flying.

He rubs his head. Looks me up and down. "You're going, aren't you? To the festival."

"None of your business."

"But it's not safe, Lonny. What if they find out—"

"They won't."

"I'm coming too."

"There's not enough time. Got to get there before they close the gates. You'll slow me down."

"No I won't." He scrambles over to the back door and stuffs his feet into his boots. "I'll keep up."

"What about the watches?"

"It's only one day." He whips his laces into bows with his quick watchmaking fingers. "We'll be back after that."

Will we?

Maybe.

I hook my rucksack over my shoulders. "Well, you'd better keep quiet, all right?" I pull open the kitchen drawer and dig out a second torch. "And you'd better keep up, too. Don't think I'm gonna slow down for you."

I chuck him the torch, then I'm out of the door and loping towards the thick dense trees.

Towards the Northgate.

Towards Erin.

Towards the only place I'll ever find out anything about my mother.

And there's Midge, running after me in his baseball cap, pushing his arms into his coat sleeves as he goes.

The dry forest ground snaps under our feet.

Jess was right. It never did start raining.

CHAPTER 18

"Wow," says Midge.

Wow.

The dandelion field is a huge pool of yellow light. Every stem glows. Every seed glimmers. The floodlights are mounted high up on the city wall and the river thrums and rumbles underneath. And what looks like pretty much the entire population of Farstoke is gathered along the outside of the wall, right next to the Northgate.

"Should we follow the road?" pants Midge. "Or just go through the dandelions?"

Can't believe he's managed to keep up with me.

I start walking. Straight for Farstoke. Giant strides

in giant boots, crushing time under my feet with every
step.

Nearly there. The night air hums with warm light and
Farstoke voices.

"Welcome one and all!" An echoey voice booms
across the field. "The moment has come for us to
begin the Lifeling Festival once more. It's time
to celebrate life, myth, miracle and magic!"
SCREEEEECH. The words twist into a metallic
scream. Midge covers his ears.

"It's the hour for all Farstokers," the voice continues,
"to pause our lives for a day, in contemplation of the
lifeling folk. We must not allow them to be forgotten,
for if we do, they might never return. So we gather
here for the annual Farstoke Lifeling Festival to
give thanks and offer gifts, so that one day, when we
need one most, a lifeling might appear for us, too."
SCREEEEEEEEECH.

I cover my ears as well this time.

"I now invite you all into the field," the voice says,
"to pick your dandelion clocks. Then I ask you to
hold them carefully, please, while I read out the first
tale. After that we will release the seeds of time into
the night, as a gift for the lifeling folk."

The Farstokers flood forward into the glowing field.
Children, grown-ups, mums and dads, grandmas and
grandpas, all rushing in, shouting and talking and
plucking seed heads from the ground. The moonlit

stag towers above them, keeping watch.

"D'you think we should pick some too?" says Midge. "Just so we look like everyone else?"

Yeah. He's right, I s'pose.

I pick two dandelion clocks. Midge grabs two whole handfuls.

We carry on towards the crowd.

Yap! Yap-yap!

Great. It's Suki. That's all I need.

She gallops towards us, her luminous pink collar reflecting brightly under the lights. She skids to her usual cowardly halt a few metres in front of me.

"Suki! Suki! Come back." It's Katy, squeezing through the people. "Oh – Midge! Midge and Lonny!"

Grrrrrrrrrrr.

"Shush, Suki. Bad girl! Lonny's our friend." Katy hurls herself at Midge and gives him a huge hug. He holds his dandelions out to the side to stop them getting squashed.

"I can't believe you came!" Katy scoops up the growling Suki. "We're going to have *so much fun.* Come on!"

I follow as she weaves through the crowd to Jess and Erin, dragging Midge by the hand.

"Midge!" says Jess. "And Lonny! How wonderful!"

"Hi," says Erin. She smiles, just a little.

Jess takes Midge's hands in hers. "I was worried about you. Was everything OK at home?"

"It's all fine," I tell her.

She tilts Midge's cap back to see him better. "You're going to have the most brilliant time, Midge Quicke."

Grrrrrrrrrrrrrrrr. Suki shows me her teeth.

"OK, are we all ready?" says the echoey voice. *SCREEEEEEEEEECH.*

"Yes!" shouts the crowd.

I see who's making the speech and the screeching now. It's David from Farstoke Groceries talking through a big cone-shaped thing. A *megaphone*, I think.

"Then settle down," he says. "Find a comfortable spot with your dandelions and your family. I'm going to tell you a story."

The Farstokers whoop and cheer, then they all start to spread out rugs and unfold canvas chairs.

Jess pulls something out of her bag. "Here, I brought a blanket. It's got rather a lot of Waldo's hair on it, I'm afraid, but it's better than nothing."

She flaps out the blanket. Suki sniffs at it.

Yap! Yap-yap!

Me and Erin pull the corners to make it flat.

I sit down with Midge, Katy, Erin, Jess and all the seed heads we've picked. Dandelions and family. Feels more like family than anything at home right now anyway.

Maybe Jess is right. Maybe I really do belong here.

Suki curls into Erin's lap. She keeps her little eyes fixed on me all the time.

CHAPTER 19

I'm going to tell you a story. A true story. From way, way back in the days before cars or lorries or aeroplanes, when everyone went around on juddering pushbikes or snorting, stamping ponies and you had to wind up your wristwatch every single day or you'd get lost in time.

Way back then, there lived a gentleman called Mr Louis Edward Sinkly. Mr Louis Edward Sinkly lived in the town of Farstoke, which was far away from anywhere else in the world. Farstoke had been there for as long as anyone could remember, and a lot longer than that. It had a Northgate, and a Southgate, and an Eastgate and a Westgate. And just east of

the Westgate stood a very large house called Sinkly Manor, which was Mr Louis Edward Sinkly's home. The Sinkly family had amassed a fortune from button manufacturing, and they always spent generously for the good of the whole town.

Indeed, right in the middle of Farstoke – south of the Northgate and east of the Westgate – the Sinklys had built a tall clock tower, and gifted it to the people of Farstoke to enjoy for evermore. Every winter the hands of the clock sagged under the weight of winking, glinting snow, and every summer they creaked and stretched in the smile of the sun.

It was beneath that clock that our Mr Louis Edward Sinkly had the very good fortune of meeting a young lady by the name of Freida. He took her for his wife, and she bore him two beautiful children. They named them Gordon and Gordana. Gordon and Gordana were the apples of their parents' eyes. They were their strawberries and cream, their teacakes and jam. In short, the children were perfect, and Mr Louis Edward Sinkly thought himself the happiest man in the whole world. But one day, when Gordon was just ten and Gordana only eight, the pair snuck out from the town and came across a nest of adders in the meadows beyond the Westgate.

Gordana poked at the snakes with a stick, and one slithered forward and bit into her brother's ankle.

The venom took quick effect. Gordon's ankle swelled up, then his calf, then his thigh, then his belly.

A bright blotchy rash raced across his skin until his lips grew thick and his breath grew weak.

Little Gordana had to do something. She ran across the meadow, flew in under the Westgate and hollered for help.

A hand touched her shoulder. Can you guess who it was?

It was a lifeling! A lifeling boy! Come to her when she needed him the most. She'd never seen one in real life, only heard about them in stories, but she instantly knew him for what he was. Something about his tiny frame, his willowy arms, his fine-boned hands. She knew it in her heart.

"Quick," said the lifeling boy. He was jumpy, agitated. He rubbed at his jawbone. "I'll save your brother. Quick. Quick!"

They ran together back to Gordon, who was gasping his last.

The lifeling boy touched Gordon's cheek. Only the tips of his fingers made contact. And the life flowed back into Gordon, right in front of his sister's open-wide eyes.

His breathing deepened, his rash vanished, his swelling calmed.

"Gordon! Gordana!"

Louis and Freida were running across the meadows towards them. "What's wrong?" they called. "Mrs Edmunton heard you at the gate. Is that Gordon? Is he all right?"

Gordon sat up and brushed the meadowsweet out from his hair. "It's OK," he said. "I'm fine."

Louis fell to his knees and cupped the precious boy's face in his hands. "What happened?"

"He got saved." Gordana looked up at the lifeling boy. But he wasn't a boy any more. He was an old man, crinkled and bent and tremored – all the life drawn out of him and sucked into Gordon. "He got saved by the lifeling," she said.

Mr Louis Edward Sinkly took his family safely home. And he took the old lifeling man too, and cared for him until his death, which wasn't very long at all, as he'd given his own days away in return for dear Gordon's. When the lifeling died, Mr Louis Edward Sinkly gave him a funeral just as fine as any he'd have planned for himself.

And that's why we celebrate the Lifeling Festival – to give thanks and offer gifts, so that one day, when we need one most, a lifeling might appear for us, too.

CHAPTER 20

"…and there ends our first lifeling story of this year's festival." *SCREEEEEEEECH.* "We've not long now before midnight and the Closing of the Gates, so if you'd all like to stand up…"

Everyone mumbles and rustles and gets to their feet.

"Lonny?" Midge tugs at my sleeve.

"…hold up your dandelion clocks…"

Everyone lifts their dandelions.

"Lonny?" Tug, tug, tug. "Their stories are—"

"Shhh," I say.

"…take a deep breath…"

We all breathe in.

"…and offer those seeds of time to the lifeling folk!"

Whhhhhhhhhhhhhhhhhh!

Everyone blows.

Everyone blows and a million trillion dandelion seeds drift into the floodlit air. A million trillion specks of life. Yellow and white and gold.

Farstoke stands silent. Time floats and bobs and turns and twists like there's no such thing as gravity at all.

"Wow," whispers Midge.

"The festival has truly begun," says David through the megaphone. "And now it's time to go back into Farstoke –" *SCREEEEEEEECH* – "for the Closing of the Gates!"

The whole crowd claps and stamps. We drop our stalks to the ground, gather up the blanket and join the mass of people funnelling back in through the Northgate.

"Lonny?" Tug, tug, tug.

"What? Get off my arm."

"That story," he whispers. "It's different from ours. Different from Grandma Quicke's."

I know. I don't need blinkin' Midge to tell me. I heard for myself.

"Get off." I yank my sleeve out of his grip.

"But, Lonny, maybe this isn't such a good idea after all. What if—"

Midge stops, because everyone's started to sing.

"I'll sing you one, oh.
Green grow the rushes, oh!

136

What is your one, oh?
One is one and all alone and evermore shall be so."
It feels like the whole world is right here, shuffling under the Northgate at midnight, singing this song.
"I'll sing you four, oh.
Green grow the rushes, oh!
What are your four, oh?
Four for the Gospel makers."
I kind of remember it from a million years ago, but not really properly. And I can't quite catch all the words, but the Farstokers know it all the way through. Sometimes they stamp their feet, and sometimes only the women are singing, and sometimes everyone goes loud and sometimes everyone goes soft and I just can't seem to figure it out at all.

Half of the crowd is already back into Farstoke. Me and Midge and Erin and Katy and Jess are getting nearer and nearer and nearer to the gate.

"Lonny?" Tug, tug, tug. "I don't think we should go in. They're gonna close the gates and we won't be able to get back out again. Did you hear that story? Did you listen to it, Lonny?"

"Get off me, Midge." I stumble in the dark grass. "Shut up about the stories. I don't care. I don't care about any of them. You do whatever you want. I'm going into Farstoke."

"Midge? Are you OK?" Jess jostles her way across to him. "You must be getting tired – it's so late. Come on. I've got plenty of duvets and pillows; we'll make you up a nice bed." She wraps her arm round his shoulders and herds him forward. "I've got cocoa and biscuits too. D'you like cocoa?"

And we move with the singing, stamping, shuffling crowd, under the stag and into the town. Right past the place where my mother stood with her scarf and her friend and her *LIFE LING* T-shirt.

When we reach the end of the song and everyone's inside the gate, David from Farstoke Groceries passes the megaphone to Daniel.

"Farstokers," says Daniel. "It's time for the countdown. All together now!"

TEN!

NINE!

EIGHT!

SEVEN!

Eight men – four on the left, four on the right – lean into the massive wooden doors on either side of the gate. They push them towards each other.

CREEEEEEEEEEEEEEEEEEAK.

SIX!

FIVE!

FOUR!

They meet right in the middle of the road, and the dandelion field and the forest disappear from sight.

THREE!

TWO!

An iron locking bar is lifted into place.

ONE!

The crowd cheers and whoops and whistles.

"Do we go round and close the other gates after this?" I say.

"No," laughs Katy. "Course not! All the gates shut at midnight, all at once. We come and watch this one, though, because of the dandelions."

All four gates closed.

No one's coming in, and no one's going out. Not for a whole twenty-four hours.

Like a spell on the town.

Part 2:
FESTIVAL

CHAPTER 21

"I wasn't even in Farstoke that long ago, my love."
The lady on the stall picks up a T-shirt that's been
dumped in a heap. She shakes it out and folds it up.
"You might try Bernie – he usually sets up shop at the
Southgate, near the zip wire."

We're in Sinkly Square, under the canopy. The
green ribbons have been pulled out from the pole in
all directions and fixed around the buildings, so the
whole thing has become a living, rippling ceiling.
Sunlight streams through it, casting stripes over our
faces.

We've already tried two other stalls. No one
remembers my mother.

Grrrrrrrrrrrrrrr.

"Don't worry, Lonny." Erin yanks Suki away from me with her luminous pink lead. "I'm pretty sure there'll be more at the Eastgate and Westgate too."

Every time I turn back round there seem to be even more people in Sinkly Square. Pushing and shoving and queuing and shouting and chatting and eating and fussing. And every single person here is dressed in green. Green hats and dresses and trousers and coats. Green T-shirts and shoes and jackets and scarves. Babies zipped and poppered into green all-in-ones. Toddlers running about in green wellies. And when we left the house Jess was still there, painting green varnish on to her fingernails.

Grrrrrrrrrrrrrrrrrrrrr.

"Suki!" says Katy. "Stop growling! She really doesn't like you, does she, Lonny?"

I'm not that keen on her, either, to be honest, but I don't say it out loud. I roll up the cuffs of the huge green jumper Katy insisted I put on. It's too big, even for me. Makes a change, though, I s'pose, from wearing stuff that's too small.

Katy's in her lifeling outfit – leafy tunic, glittering cloak. No idea why they think that's what a lifeling looks like, but that's another thing I'm not going to be saying out loud.

Yap! Yap-Yap!

Midge crouches down to stroke Suki.

"Sukes is in the doghouse today with Dad," says

Erin. "When we got back last night she found a bit of pizza Katy had left lying around. She gobbled it down and threw up all over the hall floor. Then this morning she got into Gran's garden again but luckily we found out before you lot noticed. Think Gran's getting pretty fed up with it. Anyway, Dad said we had to keep her out of the house today or he can't be held responsible for his actions."

"Poor Suki," says Katy. "Not her fault if she likes the smell of Waldo. And pizza."

Suki licks Midge's face. "I think she likes me," he says.

"She likes most people," says Erin. "Apart from Lonny."

"Rin! Rinny!" It's those girls again. Yaz and Flissie. "With your *new friends* again?" They're both holding sticks with huge green fuzzy stuff on it. It smells sweet, like sugar.

"No!" Erin's face goes red. "My dad said I had to look after them today, that's all. They've never been to the festival before. They don't know their way around Farstoke."

Yaz and Flissie giggle. They pull off bits of the fuzzy stuff and pop it into their mouths. "S'OK, Rinny, we understand. You'd much rather spend the day with your boyfriend than hang around with us."

"No, I wouldn't! And he's not my boyfriend."

Katy rolls her eyes. "I'd better be going," she says. "It's nearly ten o'clock. Next time you see me I'll be at the front of the procession."

She slips off into the crowd, cloak twinkling behind her.

"Hey." Yaz or Flissie points down at Midge. "My mum saw that kid last night at the ceremony. She said he looks just like a lifeling. And she's right – he really does. Look, Fliss – he's just like the pictures. And he looks so cute in that festival T-shirt! Hey, can we get a selfie with you, little lifeling boy?"

Midge stands up. "What's a selfie?"

The girls look at each other, then burst into laughter. "You don't know what a selfie is? Rinny, where on earth did you *find* these boys? Here – hold our candyfloss, would you?"

They both shove their fuzzy green sticks towards Erin and pull mobile phones out of their pockets. They arrange Midge in between them, whip his hat off and hold their phones out at arm's length.

Erin's fumbling with the two sticks and Suki's lead.

"D'you want me to take Suki?" I say.

"Thanks." She passes me the lead.

Yaz and Flissie pucker up their lips and take backwards photos of themselves. Midge looks bewildered in the middle.

"You can go with them if you want to." I say it quiet, so only Erin can hear. "It's fine. Me and Midge don't really need looking after."

She scratches the back of her hand.

"Oh!" Yaz – no, *Flissie* – looks up from her phone.

"Sorry, Rin, I forgot to ask. How's your mum?"

Erin glances up at number 119 behind us. Her mum's bedroom window looks out over the square. "She's not too good today. She won't be coming out for the festival. She's with Dad at home. I'm worried that we exhausted her yester—"

"Oh, that's a shame," says Yaz. "But I'm sure she'll be all right again soon."

"Yeah, she'll be fine again soon." Flissie sticks Midge's hat back on his head. "When my mum got the flu she was in bed for two whole weeks! We had to do all the washing and clean the toilets and everything. But she was all right in the end."

"Clean the toilets?" says Yaz. "Yuck!"

"It *was* yuck." Flissie pulls a face. "Are you having to clean the toilets, Rin?"

"Well." Erin blinks back tears. "No, I mean, my dad and my gran are—"

DONG.

"It's ten o'clock!" Yaz and Flissie grab each other's shoulders and jump up and down.

DONG.

"Procession's starting!" They grab their candyfloss. "Let's go and get a good spot near the front! You coming, Rin?"

DONG.

Erin scratches her hand some more.

DONG.

"You go," I tell her. "I'm fine. You don't need to—"

"No," she says. "I'm staying here. With you and Midge."

DONG.

"Ahhh – staying with Lonny?" The girls giggle. They pucker up their lips and make kissing sounds. "All right, then – see you later! Bye, Erin! Bye, Erin's boyfriend! Bye, little lifeling boy!" They squeeze back into the crowd, holding their candyfloss up above their heads.

DONG.

Midge ducks back down to stroke Suki again.

DONG.

Erin pulls her green shirt cuffs over her sore hands. "I'm sorry," she says to me.

"What for?"

DONG.

"They're all right, really." She scuffs the ground with the toes of her shoes.

"I know."

"It's just that they don't understand. About Mum. That's all."

No. I do, though.

DONG.

I understand.

DONG.

"What's that?" Midge stands up. "I can hear music."

"Oh, it's the recorders," says Erin. "It's starting. The procession's starting!"

CHAPTER 22

"Back up! Back up!" A woman dressed head to toe in the brightest green I've ever seen pushes through the people, gesturing at us all to stand back. "Make way for the lifeling!" she shouts.

We all shuffle backwards and a pathway forms, with green-clothed Farstokers lining each side. It leads past Jess's house, past the Vosses' house and away from Sinkly Square. I lean forward and look up the pathway to where the music's coming from.

There she is. Katy.

Her green cape shimmers out behind her and a ring of woven flowers sits on her head. She walks slowly towards us, chin held high and mouth squeezed tight,

like she might burst with smiling if she doesn't hold it in. Behind her are David and Daniel from Farstoke Groceries in matching green jackets and trousers. They've got the megaphone again. And behind them are the musicians. There must be thirty of them? Forty? Fifty? All playing recorders – some large, some tiny.

The crowd starts to sing. I recognise the song from when I was little.

"My grandfather's clock was too tall for the shelf
So it stood ninety years on the floor."

More and more voices join the singing.

"It was taller by half than the old man himself
Though it weighed not a penny-weight more."

Underneath the small high recorders are the lower ones, keeping time.

Tick. Tock. Tick. Tock. Tick. Tock. Tick. Tock.

Nice and steady.

"It was bought on the morn of the day that he was born.

It was always his pleasure and pride."

Katy's getting closer. She'll be able to see us soon.

Tick. Tock. Tick. Tock. Tick. Tock. Tick. Tock.

But she doesn't look at us. She keeps her chin lifted. She keeps smiling. Her cloak ripples and winks.

"But the clock stopped, never to go again,
When the old man died."

She walks past – steady, steady, steady – as the next verse starts.

David and Daniel follow her, then the recorder players, and after that the crowd folds in behind them, and we all become a moving, living, singing procession. We're drawn along, out of Sinkly Square and into the winding streets of the spellbound town.

The morning chases past in a Farstoke riot of music and market stalls and street performers. Stags and wolves and geese and bears. Songs I almost know but don't remember learning. Stories that are nearly the same as the ones I've known forever. And lifelings *everywhere* – on hats and badges and T-shirts and flags and posters and cakes. Jess is right. Farstoke really does love a lifeling. By the time we reach the last gate – the Southgate – I'm almost hoping one will appear myself.

The Southgate statue is a goose, wings spread wide and neck outstretched. And the river's right nearby, just like at the Northgate, but here it's rumbling out of the town rather than in.

And there, strung across the water, is Katy's zip wire. It's higher than I thought it'd be – almost as high as the town walls. A tall platform stands at one end of it, on the far side of the river. Safety gates have been put across the middle of the bridge to stop everyone pouring over.

The recorder players are still going strong. Their notes bob and float on the air, like mayflies. Like dandelion seeds.

"I'll sing you one, Oh.
Green grow the rushes, Oh!
What is your one, Oh?
One is one and all alone and evermore shall be so."
It's the same song they sang last night.

Erin stands on her tiptoes and tries to see between people's heads. "I know we haven't had much luck with the T-shirts so far, Lonny," she says, "but I'm pretty sure there'll be another stall around here somewhere."

"Erin! Midge! Lonny!" Katy squeezes through the crowd. Her flower crown is wonky on her head. "This is totally my favourite song. Lonny and Midge, listen – you don't sing the threes all right? Only girls sing the threes. You do the twos, then we all do the hi-ho. Get it?"

Katy and Erin start singing, loud as they can.

Yap! Yap-yap! Suki joins in too.

I listen. It's true. Every time they get to three the men go quiet. The women sing – *"Three! Three! The ri-i-i-i-vals!"* – their voices climbing up a scale. Then the men and boys crash in. The words become punches in the air. *"Two! Two! The lily-white boys, all dressed up in green –"*

And then all together for a foot-stomping, ground-shuddering *"HI-HO!"*

And everyone, quieter now: *"One is one and all alone and evermore shall be so."*

And even though last night I couldn't catch the

words and didn't get the actions, this time it all comes to me just like magic and I'm joining in too – laughing when Erin and Katy sing the threes, then booming out the twos with the men. Our melded voices vibrate my ribs. They shake up my atoms. They fuse me into Farstoke.

"Katy – Katy Voss!" It's Daniel. He nods towards the zip wire and the gated-off bridge. "Time for your *pièce de résistance.*"

"The zip wire!" Katy pushes her flower crown up on one side but now it's just wonky in the other direction. "Watch me go across, Midge. It's the best thing in the world. And afterwards you can do it too."

Midge looks at the zip wire, and the platform, and the river underneath. "I'm not sure I really—"

"Oh, you have to do it, Midge – it's brilliant."

We watch as Katy gets led over the bridge and clipped into a harness. The recorders start up a new tune.

"*Oranges and lemons, say the bells of St Clement's.*
You owe me five farthings, say the bells of St Martin's."

Katy starts climbing a ladder that reaches all the way up to the top of the platform.

"*When will you pay me? say the bells of Old Bailey.*
When I grow rich, say the bells of Shoreditch.
When will that be? say the bells of Stepney.
I do not know, says the great bell of Bow."

She's nearly at the top. Sunshine splashes over the

water below her.

"Here comes a candle to light you to bed.

Here comes a chopper to chop off your head."

She's there. They clip her harness to the wire.

It's windy up there. Her hair and her cloak curl and roll and her flower crown blows clean off. Katy makes a grab for it. The platform wobbles – Katy stumbles – but the harness holds her tight.

The crown drifts down, down, down, into the river.

Katy sets herself steady.

"LIFELING!" the crowd cheers.

Katy waves, and we go even wilder.

"Phew," says David through his megaphone. "OK, Farstoke – are you ready for the final story of the day?"

CHAPTER 23

A long, long time ago – millions of lifetimes ago – there was a place called Farstoke. This was long before the clock tower was built, and long before the Sinklys even thought of making a single button, but the river still ran through it as fast and as wide as it does today, and the city walls were young and strong.

Farstoke could be entered by one of its four gates: the Northgate, the Southgate, the Eastgate or the Westgate, and each gate was guarded by a different creature. Stags roamed outside the Northgate, antlers ready to butt and battle any enemy who might approach. Wolves prowled the Eastgate, baring shiv-sharp teeth. Bears dozed in front of the Westgate with

one eye open – ready to wake in a wink of a second and take you out with one swipe of a heavy clawed paw. And geese guarded the Southgate – perhaps the best watchmen of them all, for no one gets past a goose gaggle without every person in town being alerted to their presence, and there's no animal more dangerous than a human, as we all well know.

In Farstoke there lived a little boy called William Memrie. William didn't get on with the other Farstoke children, but he did love animals. He loved the horse his father rode to and from the city on; he loved the cat his mother kept to ward off the rats; he even loved the rats. Some said William could talk with the animals as well as St Francis himself.

And William also loved the gate animals. He would slip outside the Northgate when he should be at school, stolen apples in his pockets, and the stags would eat from his very hands. He spoke to the Southgate geese in their own language, flapping and honking and pecking, and they welcomed him with open wings. He would even ride atop the grizzly bears at the Westgate, gripping on to the thick velvety skin on the scruff of their necks to stay on.

But William's favourite animals of them all were the wolves. It's told he would creep past the Eastgate at night and curl up with the cubs, and be licked and nuzzled to sleep alongside them by their wild wolf mothers.

But this was a time of war and terror. The people

of Farstoke continually feared attack from without, which is why they kept the deadly animals guarding the gates. And one night – while William was curled up not with the wolf cubs, who were now full grown, but back at home in his own hard bed – Farstoke was attacked.

The attackers were clever. They knew about Farstoke. They knew about the gates, and the unusual animal guards. They came by stealth in the deepest of darkness. They divided themselves into four separate groups, one larger than the rest, and with a perfectly timed ambush they descended upon all four gates at exactly the same moment. Within fifteen short minutes the stags and the bears and the geese and the wolves were all defeated – dead, dying and desperate.

All except one.

The attackers weren't fools. They knew you could take on one stag, or one bear, even one wolf at a time. But they knew that the geese must be dealt with all at once or the whole town would awake. So the largest group were sent to the Southgate – and they almost succeeded. They lured the geese far from the gate and into a thick copse with well-practised false goose calls, then they set upon them all at once, one man to each bird. But a single lone goose escaped. She ran for her life, and honked as if her very existence depended on it.

Now, the people of Farstoke were used to one errant goose honking in the night. A few rolled over in their sleep, most didn't stir at all. But William heard the call – and he understood it. He knew immediately that the town was in danger. He leaped out of bed and alerted his parents. They woke the rest of the town while William ran to his animal friends.

He found the goose beyond the Southgate, shaking and shivering, and he scooped her up under his arm. Then he ran for the Eastgate to his beloved wolves.

Meanwhile the Farstokers were defending their town and – thanks to the early alert from William and the goose – they did indeed manage to save Farstoke from the night-time attackers.

At the Eastgate William discovered his wolf friends in a terrible state. Every last one was either dead already, or heaving its final breaths in the thin moonlight. William curled up with them, just like he'd done when they were cubs, and the goose curled up too for the wolves were too injured even to bother it. William fell into a fitful sleep, but was woken by a call.

"William. William." It was a soft voice, reaching through his damaged dreams. When he looked up he saw a girl – a lifeling girl! Come to help when he needed it most! He'd never seen one in real life, only heard about them in stories, but he instantly knew her for what she was. Something about her tiny frame, her willowy arms, her fine-boned hands. He knew it in his heart.

He stood aside and watched as the lifeling girl lay

her hands upon his lupine friends, saving one after another after another, until a full ten wolves were up again and prowling and the goose had to be carried once more to keep her safe.

And the lifeling wasn't a girl any more, but an old lady, crinkled and bent and tremored. William took her to his home where his mother gave her the best food and the strongest bed and the most respectable clothes they possessed, and she lived as splendidly as the finest folk in Farstoke. And upon her death she was given a grand funeral with dandelions and wallflowers and corncockles, and she was buried on the exact square of ground that would become the footprint of the clock tower hundreds of years later.

William was celebrated as the saviour of the town. He grew up to become a talented sculptor, and in memory of his animal friends he carved four huge, beautiful beasts: a stag, a bear, a goose and a wolf, and the people of Farstoke set them upon the gates so they would always remember the creatures who fell and the boy who saved the town.

And that's why we celebrate the Lifeling Festival – to give thanks and offer gifts, so that one day, when we need one most, a lifeling might appear for us, too.

CHAPTER 24

Everyone's eyes are on Katy.

Everyone's except Midge's. He yanks at my jumper. "That one was different too, Lonny. All their stories are different from ours."

"Just stop, Midge." I pull my arm away. "I've told you – *at every gate* – I don't care. Anyway, maybe their stories are right and ours are wrong. Ever thought of that, have you?"

"Suki?" Erin crouches down on the grass. "What's up, Sukes?"

Suki's stumbling around on the ground between us. Her front leg's gone rigid and shaky.

"Is there something wrong with her?" I say.

"I don't know." Erin picks her up. "Her legs are trembling."

"Maybe she's cold," says Midge.

"But it's mild today." Erin lets Suki lick her face. "What's wrong, Sukes? What is it?"

Suki scrabbles her front feet on to Erin's shoulder and licks her ear.

"She seems all right again now," I say.

"Yeah," says Erin. She twists her head away from Suki's slurping tongue. "She does, doesn't she?"

"Look," says Midge. "Katy's just about to go."

Katy's got hold of a bar hooked over the wire.

DONG.

The clock tower starts its midday strike.

DONG.

On the third strike everyone shouts TEN!

On the fourth they shout NINE!

EIGHT!

SEVEN!

SIX!

FIVE!

FOUR!

Me and Midge and Erin shout as loud as we can.

Katy squeezes hold of the bar.

THREE!

TWO!

ONE!

Katy leaps off the platform.

She flies over the river – legs swinging, cloak

flowing, hair streaming.

A thousand Farstoke arms hold up phones and cameras as she hurtles past.

She lets out a scream and – *CLACK* – the bar whacks into the stand at the other end. Her landing's softened by a stack of hay bales.

Katy stands up flush-faced and grinning the biggest grin in the world. She waves at us. "Midge! Erin! Lonny!"

We wave back.

A long queue is growing at the bridge. The second person's already being strapped into a harness and a third is being taken across the bridge to the platform.

"Did you see?" Katy runs over. "Did you see me go down?"

"Excuse me, Katy," a lady calls out. "Katy Voss?" She's got very short hair, a biro and a ring-bound notebook just like the ones Dad uses. There's another lady behind her who's got a camera hanging round her neck with a lens so long she has to hold it up all the time.

"Did it look like I was flying in to save someone?" says Katy. "Like a real lifeling? Did it?"

Why on earth do they all think lifelings can fly?

"It looked *exactly* like that." Midge's grin is as big as Katy's.

The woman with short hair catches up. "Hi. Katy Voss, isn't it? I'm Penny Hendrix, *Farstoke Gazette*, and this is Viv, our photographer."

Viv gives a little nod.

"Oh." Katy tucks a strand of hair behind her ear. "Hello."

"We got some fantastic shots of you leading the procession and coming down the zip wire," says Penny. "Any chance Viv could get a few close-ups? And maybe I could get a few words from you on what it feels like to be lifeling for the day?"

"Well, yes, OK." Katy tilts her head and smooths down her cloak. "Do I look all ri—"

"Hold on a minute." Viv lifts her camera up and points it straight past Katy. *Click, click, click.* "That's the little kid people have been talking about. The one who looks just like a lifeling. Mind if I take a few shots, lifeling boy?" She doesn't wait for an answer. *Click, click, click.*

Midge freezes. His smile's gone.

"So it is," says Penny. "What's your name, kid?"

Katy's smile's gone too. She's looking from Midge to Viv, backwards and forwards.

"Midge," whispers Midge.

"Mitch?" Penny scribbles in her notebook. "Got a surname, Mitch?"

Click, click, click.

"Hey, Katy," says Viv. "Could we borrow your cloak for a sec? I'd love to get a photo of Mitch in that – he really is the perfect lifeling. Should've had him leading the procession, shouldn't we, Pen?"

Click, click, click.

"Ha!" says Penny. "Yeah." She fiddles with the cloak button under Katy's chin.

"But, but…" Katy grips the collar of the cloak, holding it tight round her neck. "Erin? I think maybe I should keep the cloak on, don't you? I mean, I won the vote and everything."

"What?" Erin mumbles. She's not even looking. She's crouched down again with her back to us.

"I said d'you think maybe it should be me who keeps the cloak on, because—"

"I don't have time, Katy," Erin snaps. "Can't you see I'm busy? Suki's sick. Just make a decision yourself for once."

I look over Erin's shoulder. Suki's thrown up on the grass. It's got streaks of blood in it.

"I know!" Viv lowers her camera. "Let's get him on the zip wire. All dressed up. I'm sure they'll let us jump the queue. Press privilege and all that."

"Super idea," says Penny. "Come on, Katy, it's only for a short time – let us borrow the cloak."

Katy looks at me.

Midge looks at me.

So suddenly *I'm* the one who has to decide?

Photos of Midge all over Farstoke? Dressed up like a lifeling?

It makes my heart kick, but that's just the old Lonny thinking.

Because, actually, it's OK.

Everything's fine.

Farstoke loves a lifeling.

All the rest has just been twisted, messed-up stories.

I shrug one shoulder. It's up to them.

Katy takes a deep breath. She smiles at Midge. "Well, all right, then. Midge is my friend. I can share." She drops her hands away from her collar.

"Way to go, Katy." Penny unbuttons the cloak.

Midge shakes his head. "You don't have to, Katy." His voice is a whisper again. "I'm fine, really. I don't even want to—"

But Penny's already whisked off the cloak. She sweeps it round Midge, buttons it up, takes off his baseball cap and shoves it in front of Katy. "Look after that, would you?" she says. Then she grabs Midge's hand and drags him off towards the bridge. Katy and Viv hurry after them.

I kneel down next to Erin.

Grrrrrrrrrrrr.

"Well, she's still managing to growl at me," I say, "so that seems pretty normal at least."

"She just chucked up." Erin ruffles Suki's ears. "Maybe she ate something funny. Maybe she just needed to be sick."

"Yeah."

"Probably got it out of her system now." Erin stands up. "OK, well, you know what time it is, don't you?"

"Just after twelve?"

"Nope." She smiles. "Zip wire time. Come on!"

CHAPTER 25

We watch Midge from the end of the queue. Takes them ages to get him up there.

For heaven's sake, Midge, just get on with it.

When he finally gets to the top, the crowd cheer for him. "*Life-ling! Life-ling! Life-ling!*" The assistant hooks his harness over the bar. Now she's pointing at the bar and nodding. I can just imagine the conversation.

"Just hold on, that's all you've got to do."

"Yes, I know, but—"

"Put your hands here, like Katy did."

"Yes, I saw Katy, but what if I fa—"

"You can't fall, that's why we have the harness."

"Yes, but I don't like the water and—"

He's always got a *but*, Midge has. Always some excuse for being a chicken.

"Life-ling! Life-ling! Life-ling!"

Just do it, Midge.

Don't you see? It's flying. *Flying.* When are you ever going to get to do that again?

Erin's shouting with the rest of the crowd. *"Life-ling! Life-ling! Life-ling!"*

Suddenly he's got both hands on the bar and the assistant doesn't mess around. She gives him a hefty shove between the shoulder blades and he's off.

The crowd roars.

The cloak ripples behind him.

And, for half a minute, it's Midge who's the lifeling instead of me.

Then – CLACK – he whacks into the hay bales.

"Erin?" I say. "Can I show you something?"

"Course. What is it?"

I take my rucksack off my shoulders and pull out my map. It's even more crumpled and creased than it was before, but I don't care. I open it out, so we can see Prague, Versailles, London. "Have you ever been to any of these places? The ones I've circled? My mum visited them all. I've got – well, I *had* – photographs."

A breeze catches the map and the top flaps over. Erin unflaps it, holds it still. "I've been to London," she says.

"I'm going one day," I tell her. "To all of them. Just

like my mum did. No one's going to stop me."

She runs her fingers over the tatty old map. Edinburgh, Amsterdam, Paris, Berlin. Her hair blows in front of her face.

"Maybe … maybe you'd like to come too," I say.

"Erin! Lonny!" Midge and Katy spot us in the queue. "Did you see Midge go down? Did you see him?"

I fold the map up quickly, any old how. Shove it back into my bag.

"Course we saw him," says Erin. "And I see you've got your cloak back now, too."

"Yeah," says Katy. "I didn't mind lending it to Midge. He *did* look good in it, didn't he?"

"Yeah. But so do you."

Katy grins.

"The zip wire's brilliant, Lon." Midge looks weird. Not very Midge-like. "It's really brilliant." His hair's a sweaty mess and his skin's all pinkish. "And Katy says they're keeping it here for a whole two weeks, so can we come back and go on it again?"

"Go on it again?" I say. "They had to push you off."

"They won't have to next time, though. Next time I'll jump straight off, just like Katy did."

"Yeah!" Katy jumps up and down. "Just like I did!"

Midge jumps up and down too.

But he's not supposed to enjoy it here. He's supposed to want to be back in the forest. In the workshop. Hidden away.

It was *me* who decided to come to Farstoke. It was *my* idea. Why does he always take everything away from me?

"Yeah, right," I say. "I'll believe it when I see it."

My turn.

Harness hooked.

Handles gripped.

It's higher than it looks, when you're up here.

The river swirls below.

The ground spins.

The ladder I climbed up on is starting to look like a very good way to get down again too.

You got to do it, though, Lonny. You got to fly. I mean, Midge did it, didn't he?

And Katy. And Erin.

You got to do it.

I take a breath in and ... step off.

WHOOOOOOOSH!

The world sweeps past.

Walls.

Goose.

Wings.

River.

Sun.

Sky.

LIFE.

My mouth opens.

Scream?

No.

Laugh.

I laugh and laugh and laugh and the wind gushes into my mouth and –

CLACK.

I swing forwards – backwards – forwards – and I'm down.

They unhook me.

I take some staggery steps.

I flew.

Me, Lonny Quicke.

I flew. Like a swooping sparrowhawk.

Midge was right. It really was brilliant.

I never thought I'd get to do anything like that. Never in a billion years.

Next time I'll jump straight off too. Just like Katy.

Just like Midge.

"Hey!" I call out to the others. They're huddled round, heads together. "Hey! Did you see me flying? Shall we queue up again? That was the best thing ever." I hold out my arms, fingers wide. Feel the Farstoke breeze on my face and my neck and my chicken-sorting, boot-stuffing hands.

I am alive.

I am free.

I am exactly where I want to be.

Katy and Midge look up. Frowning. Worried.

They turn back to their huddle.

"What's up?" I jog over. "What's wrong?"

"It's Suki," says Katy. "She's sick. Really, really sick."

Erin's cross-legged on the grass. The little dog's cradled in her lap.

It's true. Something's badly wrong.

Suki's not quivering now – she's jerking. Like the hens. Like Dixon.

Her eyes roll. Bubbles of foam erupt at the corners of her mouth.

Vvvvvvmmmmm

No.

No.

No.

Not now.

I press my fingers hard against my tingling lips.

Not now, you silly, quivery, cowardly dog.

Not now.

CHAPTER 26

"Dad? Gran?" Katy bursts in through the front door of number 119 and holds it open for Erin. Weeping, stumbling, dog-carrying Erin.

"Suki's sick! Suki's sick!" shouts Katy.

Vvvvvmmmmmmmmmm

The roots of my teeth.

The thick of my tongue.

"Lonny," Midge whispers. "Lonny, don't go in! You've got to walk away."

Walk away.

Walk away.

I don't, though. I follow Katy and Erin straight into the house.

Midge scampers in after me.

"Keep your voices down." Mr Voss leans over the banister from the floor above. "Your mother's sleeping."

Jess comes out of the kitchen. "What on earth's going on?"

"It's Suki, she's—"

"I'm sorry, girls, but you're really going to have to be very quiet indeed today." *Tap-tap-tap-tap-tap*. Mr Voss's footsteps spiral down towards us. "Either that or stay outside. Your mother's not very well at all and from what I've just heard you lot may well have something to do with it. I understand you took her outside yesterday without even—"

"Dad! It's Suki – look." Katy points at the collapsed heap in Erin's arms.

Erin's eyes are blotchy with tears. The front bit of her hair is stuck to her wet face.

Jess rushes over.

Vvvvvvvvvvvvmmmmmmmmmmmmmmm

I press my fingertips into the sides of my jaw. Open and close my mouth.

Vvvvvvvvvvvvvvvvvvmmmmmmmmmmmmmm

"Oh no, oh no. I just remembered. It's my fault, isn't it?" says Katy. "I left that pizza out and she shouldn't have eaten it." Her eyes glisten up.

Jess runs gentle hands over the little dog. Celia-driving, honey-spreading hands. Her green fingernails show up bright against Suki's white coat. "A little bit of pizza wouldn't do this, Katy, love. This is something different. Erin, bring Suki into the kitchen. Put her down in her basket." She holds the kitchen door open for Erin. "Lonny?"

Vvvvvvvvvvvvvvvvvvvvvvvvmmmmmmmmmmmm

My skull thrums.

"Lonny?" she says again.

"Um … yes?"

"Phil said Suki got into the garden this morning. That rat poison from yesterday – you did put it away, didn't you? Back in the cupboard?"

The Rat-Out. Pellets all over the flower bed.

Vvvvvvvvvvvvvvvvvvvvvvvvvmmmmmmmmmmmm

The backs of my eyes. The pit of my neck.

"Um … yes. I did." Blinkin' dog, digging under the fence. Sniffing around. Getting itself into trouble. Blinkin' little sick, dying dog. "But I might have dropped some."

"You *might* have?"

"I did. I did drop some. I tried to pick it up but—"

"Phil?" Jess helps Erin settle Suki into the basket. "You need to call a vet. That stuff won't just kill rats – it'll kill pretty much anything. And for heaven's sake we've got to figure out some way of stopping her digging under the fence in future."

"Oh. Yes." Mr Voss shakes his head like he's just come out of a daze. "Of course. A vet."

It's not Katy's fault. It's mine.

First the chickens. Now Suki.

"I can see what you're thinking, Lonny Quicke," says Jess, "and you're wrong. It's not your fault – so you can stop thinking that right now, OK?"

She glances at Midge. Midge, who's standing next to a crying, fretting Katy. Midge, who's holding Katy's hand. Just to try and make her feel better.

Vvvvvvvvvvvvvvvvvvvvvvvvmmmmmmmmmmm

Mr Voss has got the telephone jammed against his ear with his shoulder. He fumbles around in the kitchen drawer. "The number's in here somewhere."

Vvvvvvvvvvvvvvvvvvvvvvvvmmmmmmmmmmm

Suki's in her basket. Staring eyes, juddering limbs. She keeps trying to lift her head up but she can't manage. Erin and Katy are on the floor close to her. The buzzing's pulling me in but I stay back here with Midge. I press my palms against the wall behind me.

Vvvvvvvvvvvvvvvvvvvvvvvvvmmmmmmmmmmm

Jess takes a towel from the radiator. She folds it up and tucks it under Suki's head. It doesn't exactly calm her down, but it stops her trying to strain her head up.

"Here it is." Mr Voss waves a small piece of paper in the air.

Bip. Bip-bip. Bip. He starts punching the number into the phone.

"What about the gates?" says Katy. "The vets aren't

in Farstoke, are they? Will they open the gates for them?"

Silence.

Mr Voss lets the phone fall to his side.

"They'll have to open them," says Erin. "They'll have to. She's sick!"

"Oh, my poor love." Jess touches her shoulder.

Erin shrugs her away. "They'll have to! It's just a stupid festival. Make-believe. Suki's *real*. They'll open the gates – won't they, Dad? You'll make them, won't you?"

"I, um." Mr Voss drops the piece of paper back into the drawer. "I don't know. I mean, we can't—"

"Call the vet, Dad! Make them open a gate! She's dying!"

"Erin, love," says Jess, "you know we don't open the gates during the festival. Maybe Suki's not as bad as you think. Maybe she'll start to get better soon all by herself."

Vvvvvvvvvvvvvvvvvvvvvvvvvvvvmmmmmmmmm

Walk away, Lonny. Walk away.

The buzzing pulls at my head, my ribs, my arms. Tries to peel me off the wall.

Vvvvvvvvvvvvvvvvvvvvvvvvvvvvmmmmmmmmm

"She won't get better. Erin's right." It's Midge. He's staring at me. "Suki's dying."

"See!" says Erin. "Even Midge can see it."

Jess presses her hands to her mouth. "Um, Lonny," she says, "I think perhaps you ought to take Midge now and leave. We'll deal with this ourselves. Go and enjoy the festival and—"

"Gran!" Erin's shaking all over. "Suki's *dying*. We've got to do something! Dad! Do something! I know, speak to David or Daniel – maybe they can—"

"Stop!" Mr Voss bangs the kitchen table. "Just stop, Erin. I can't do this now. I can't deal with it. I've got your mother upstairs – I've never seen her so ill; she's become much worse since yesterday. And I'm sure Suki'll be OK. I just—"

"Is Mum going to die?" Katy's voice has gone quiet, like Midge's. *Tick, tick, tick, tick, tick* goes the kitchen clock. "Are they both going to die?"

Suki jolts. Her breaths are noisy and jagged.

VVVVVVVVVVVVVVMMMMMMMMMMMM

"Do something!" screams Erin. "Do something!"

"Maybe we should make her throw up again," says Jess. "Lonny – you and Midge go and enjoy the festival and we'll see if we can—"

"Let me through." I push between Erin and Katy and drop down in front of the basket.

"Lonny?" say Midge. "Don't, Lonny."

VVVVVVVVVVVVVVVVVMMMMMMMMMM

My ribs vibrate. My liver, my heart, my lungs.

Tick, tick, tick, tick, tick.

"Lonny?" says Jess. "What are you doing?"

"It's all right." I give Erin a calm smile. "You don't need to worry. I can fix this."

"Stop!" Midge darts forward and yanks at my huge

green jumper. Might as well be a field mouse yanking at me.

"Stop him, someone," says Midge. Yank, yank, yank. "Stop him!"

"Midge, keep away," says Jess. "Keep away from Suki."

"Lonny?" says Mr Voss. "Are you all right?"

VVVVVVVVVVVVVVVVVVMMMMMMMM

"Stop him!" shouts Midge.

I twist round and grip his arms tight. "You're the one who's got to stop, Midge. Everything's all right – don't you see? Everything's fine. These are our friends." I look at Erin, Katy, Jess. "Isn't that right?"

Katy gives me the tiniest nod.

Erin frowns.

"Of course we're friends, Lonny," says Jess. "That's exactly why I need you to take your brother right now and—"

"See?" I squeeze Midge even harder. "Farstoke *loves* a lifeling."

I release his arms and reach forward to Suki.

I stroke her ear. Feels soft. And warm.

Kisses. Kind words.

VVVVVVVVVVVVVVVVVVMMMMMMMM

The buzzing bleeds from my shoulders into my arms, through my hands, out of my fingertips.

Suki softens. Quietens. Calms.

She blinks a watery eye.

Slurps a pale, pink tongue round her lips.

I sit back.
Breathe.
Breathe.
Breathe.
I shift my jaw from side to side. The buzzing's gone.
Silence.
Suki gets to her feet, gives herself a shake, patters out of her basket and licks my hand.
DONG.
The clock tower chimes.
One o'clock.

CHAPTER 27

"What, um…?" Mr Voss loosens the knot of his tie. It's the same one as yesterday. Tiny fox faces. His favourite. "What just happened there?"

Yap-yap!

Erin scoops Suki into her arms. Holds her up and peers at her. "What did you do, Lonny? How did you do that?"

"He's a lifeling," Katy whispers. "A real-live lifeling. It's true, isn't it, Lonny? It's true." She pulls at the cloak fastening round her neck. "Are you a lifeling too, Midge? Is it both of you?"

"Midge?" I laugh. "Course not. He's tiny. You don't stay little very long when you're a lifeling."

"This is getting ridiculous," says Erin. "There's no such thing as a lifeling."

"But you just saw it happen," says Katy. "In front of your eyes."

Suki patters up to me and nuzzles her nose into my hand. I give her a little stroke.

"The boy's a miracle worker," says Mr Voss.

"You don't really believe all this, do you, Dad? It's nonsense. Suki just got better by herself somehow. She must've just—"

"No, Erin – Katy's right," I say. "I *am* a lifeling."

Tick, tick, tick, tick, tick.

"And I think you were right too, Jess," I carry on. "I think it was my destiny to come to Farstoke and to be here today, so I could save Suki."

"Yes!" Katy jumps up. "When we needed you most. It's just like in the stories."

"Your stories are different from ours," says Midge.

"You knew about this already, Jess?" Sweat twinkles on Mr Voss's forehead.

Jess's face has gone as milky-white as the dandelion field. "I thought it was Midge," she says.

"So you did know?"

"No! No – I didn't know. I just … *suspected*. I mean, I've suspected for years, ever since I found out there were two little boys up at the Quicke place. There used to be rumours about the Quickes having lifelings in their family line, so I thought... Well, it doesn't matter what I thought. Fact is, I shouldn't have brought you here. I'm sorry. I'll take you boys home, as soon as they open the gates."

"It's OK, Jess," I tell her. "You don't need to say sorry. It's exactly like you said. This is where I belong."

Erin stares at me. She picks up Suki again and hugs her to her chest.

"But seeing as Suki seems OK now," I say, "what I'd really like to do is get back to the Southgate. D'you want to come with me, Erin? I never managed to get to the T-shirt stall to ask about my mother's—"

"Hold on." Mr Voss takes his jacket off and hangs it over the back of a chair. "Stop right there. No one's going anywhere."

"Give me your phones." Mr Voss holds out a flat hand. His eyes skip from me to Erin to Midge to Katy.

"What?" says Erin.

"Your phones," he says. "I need them."

"Phil," says Jess, "do you really think that's necessary?"

"I don't have a phone," says Katy.

"I'm not giving you my phone," says Erin. "Why d'you want it anyway?"

"Just give me your phone, Erin! And you boys – can I have them, just for a while, please."

"We don't have phones, Mr Voss."

He rubs his forehead and squeezes his eyes tight shut for a second. "Right, well," he says, "just you, then, Erin. Jess, keep yours tucked away. I mean, can you imagine the mayhem if anyone finds out?" His eyes are still zooming about, like his mind's hurtling all over the place. "In fact," he says, "I'd better go and—" He dashes to the windows and pulls the curtains closed.

"Phil," says Jess, "I think perhaps you need to calm down."

"Erin?" He dodges back and holds out his hand again.

Erin rolls her eyes. She pulls her phone out of her pocket. "Don't know why you're worried. Even if I had that whole thing filmed I wouldn't be able to *do* anything with it, would I? We live in Farstoke, remember – the last place in the universe with no connection." She slaps it down into Mr Voss's hand.

He stuffs it into his trouser pocket. "You didn't, did you? Film it, I mean?"

"Course not! I didn't know Lonny's a lifeling. I thought that was all a load of nonsense until two minutes ago."

"OK, right, OK. Let me think." He wipes his sweaty face with his shirt cuffs. There are dark puffy bags under his eyes. "OK," he says. "This is what we're going to do. None of us is going to breathe a word of this to anyone else, all right? Not a single word. And everyone's going to stay right here, in the kitchen. Everyone apart from you, Lonny. You're coming with me. I need to, um, I need to show you something. And, Jess, get some coffee on, could you? I think I need one."

"Phil," says Jess, "I really don't think you should be—"

"Stay here with the girls, Jess." Mr Voss opens the kitchen door. "Leave this to me."

I follow him out into the hallway.

"Lonny?" Midge scrambles after us.

"Get back in the kitchen, Midge," says Mr Voss.

"I don't want to. I want to stay with Lonny."

For heaven's sake. Why does he have to be so difficult?

"Midge, it's fine," I say. "It's all fine. Stop fretting. Look at everything that's happened – the ceremony, the festival, the zip wire. Farstoke *loves* a lifeling. Just like Jess said. Isn't that right, Mr Voss?"

"Um … yes. Yes. Absolutely."

"But what about Grandma's stories?"

"Don't you get it, Midge? We've been lied to. Who knows if they're even Grandma's? Maybe Dad and Grandad made them up to keep us in the forest." I wouldn't put it past them.

"But—"

"Just go back in the kitchen, will you?"

"Lonny." It's Jess, in the kitchen doorway. "Maybe you should listen to your brother."

"Please stop interfering, Jess." Mr Voss already has a hand on the banister and one foot on the spiral staircase. "And, Midge, I need you to go back into the kitchen – *now*."

"But the stories say—"

"Midge!" Can't he just be quiet? Like he used to? "I don't care what the stories say. And if you think Dad and Grandad are so right about everything, why don't you go back to them? I'm not stopping you. I never wanted you to come last night anyway. But I'm just fine right here."

He stares at me, quivering, like Suki.

CHAPTER 28

A tale from Grandma Quicke's exercise book

A long, long time ago – millions of lifetimes ago, before anyone ever dreamed of measuring minutes with anything other than a shadow-powered sundial – there was place called Farstoke. Farstoke could be entered by one of its four gates: the Northgate, the Southgate, the Eastgate or the Westgate – and each gate was guarded by a different creature. Stags roamed outside the Northgate, antlers ready to butt and battle any enemy who might approach. Wolves prowled the Eastgate, baring shiv-sharp teeth. Bears dozed in front of the Westgate with one eye open – ready to wake in

a wink of a second and take you out with one swipe of a heavy clawed paw. And geese guarded the Southgate – perhaps the best watchmen of them all, for no one gets past a goose gaggle without every person in town being alerted to their presence, and there's no animal more dangerous than a human, as we all well know.

In Farstoke there lived a little boy called William Memrie. William didn't get on with the other Farstoke children, but he did love animals. He loved the horse his father rode to and from the city on; he loved the cat his mother kept to ward off the rats; he even loved the rats. Some said William could talk with the animals as well as St Francis himself, but others said that was nonsense and he should spend a little less time trying to talk to a cat and a little more time making friends of his own kind or what on earth was to become of him when he grew up? But it was all so long ago now that it's impossible for us to know who was right and who was wrong.

Yes, William loved horses and cats and rats, but he also loved the gate animals. It's told he would slip outside the Northgate when he should be at school, stolen apples stuffed in his pockets, and the stags would eat from his very hands. It's told he spoke to the Southgate geese in their own language, flapping and honking and pecking, and they welcomed him with open wings. It's even told he would ride atop the rugged brown bears at the Westgate, gripping on to the thick velvety skin on the scruff of their necks to stay on.

But William's favourite animals of them all were the wolves. It's told he would creep past the Eastgate at night and curl up with the cubs, and be licked and nuzzled to sleep alongside them by their wild wolf mothers.

I would be lying, however, if I told you that William had no human friends at all. He had one special friend, who went by the name of Peony Patience. William and Peony were born on the same night just hours apart, and the two of them grew up together, playing on the goat-nibbled grass that separated their families' homes. They would whisper, heads together, scabbed knees touching, using words no one else could understand even if they did get close enough to overhear. Then Peony would lift her head to the rest of the town and speak for the both of them in clear plain words – using only as many as were absolutely necessary, mind you.

But Peony had a deep, inky secret. She was a lifeling. Her family knew it, and William knew it too. He couldn't remember when he'd found out or who had told him, but he knew it was a secret that must never be let loose. Peony's life depended on it.

Peony did not have such an affinity with animals as William did. She could walk away from a dying bird if she chose to, or a half-squashed butterfly, even a drowning piglet runt on one occasion. Her mother had brought her up to value her own life and to handle her gift with gentle hands and a strong heart.

No – Peony's love was of sculpting. She made things out of mud or candle wax when she was little, and as she grew she progressed on to clay, then on to large blocks of stone whenever she could find one, chipping away until it became just as she wanted.

As the pair grew older they became no less interested in animals and sculpture and each other, and no more interested in anyone else. By the time they were teenagers they were hopelessly in love. But though this was a time of great passion and art and words and adventure, it was also a time of war and terror and blood and death. The people of Farstoke continually feared attack from without, hence the deadly animals guarding the gates.

One night – while William was curled up not with the wolf cubs, who were now full grown, but back at home in his own hard bed – Farstoke was attacked.

The attackers were clever. They had heard about Farstoke. They knew about the gates, and the unusual animal guards. They came by stealth in the deepest of darkness. They divided themselves into four separate groups, one larger than the rest, and with a perfectly timed ambush they descended upon all four gates at exactly the same moment. Within fifteen short minutes the stags and the bears and the geese and the wolves were all defeated – dead, dying and desperate.

All except one.

The attackers weren't fools. They knew you could take on one stag, or one bear, even one wolf at a time. But they knew that the geese must be dealt with all at once or the whole town would awake. So the largest group were sent to the Southgate. They lured the geese far from the gate and into a thick copse with no more noise than a few gentle false goose calls, then they set upon them all at once, one man to each bird. But a single lone goose escaped – she ducked knives and dodged boots and flapped herself away and honked as if her very life depended on it.

Now, the people of Farstoke were used to one errant goose honking in the night. A few rolled over in their sleep, most didn't stir at all. But William heard the call – and he understood it. He knew immediately that the town was in danger, for the goose was telling him exactly that.

He leaped out of bed and alerted his parents. They woke the rest of the town while William ran for the terrified goose.

He found her beyond the Southgate, shaking and shivering, and he scooped her up under his arm. Then he ran for the Eastgate to his beloved wolf friends.

Meanwhile the Farstokers defended their town and – thanks to the early alert from William and the goose – their defence proved successful. The town was saved.

At the Eastgate William discovered his wolf brothers and sisters collapsed next to their mothers and fathers, their aunts and their uncles. All were either already dead, or breathing their last lungfuls and wheezing their last whines in the thin moonlight. When Peony found William, he was curled up between two of them, the shivering goose crouched at his feet.

But, don't forget, Peony was a lifeling. "William! William!" she cried – fists clenched, teeth tight, the buzzing shaking her whole body and pulling her in all directions. Her head thumped. Her heart wept. Was it William who was injured? Her beautiful, precious William? "Are you hurt?" she said. "Are you dying?"

"Peony." William opened his eyes. "No, I'm unharmed. But the animals – look. Look at them."

Peony didn't want to look. She didn't need to. She could feel it in her blood, her bones, her roots. She could feel it in the edge of her jaw, the bowls of her eyes.

William stroked his weak lupine friends. "You have to help them, Peony," he said. "You're the only one who can. You can't let them die."

Walk away.

Walk away.

It was what Peony's mother had taught her.

Take a breath, brace your heart, walk away.

"Please, Peony – don't let them die. Not all of them. I can't bear it." William got to his feet. The goose waddled in, staying close. "For me, Peony, do it for me. If you really love me, you'll save them."

And because the buzzing was so strong, and because

she loved him so much, Peony let William lead her to wolf after wolf. She grew older and older with each life saved, and by the time she had revived ten of his wolf friends she was so ancient she had not enough life left in her to save a single one more.

When the sun rose beyond the Eastgate and the people of Farstoke began to celebrate their victory, William – his wolf friends licking at his heels – finally realised what he had done.

William cared for Peony for the rest of her life – which was not very long at all. Afterwards, he decided he could never love another, so he dedicated himself to learning her beloved art of sculpture in her memory. Unlike Peony it did not come naturally to him. He worked and worked at it for his whole life. The people of Farstoke never forgot what he had done for them, so although he was never rich, they saw to it that he always had enough to eat and a roof over his head. He never married and he had no brothers or cousins, so the Memrie family line ended with him. He did, however, leave the town a legacy. Over many years he sculpted four huge and beautiful stone animals – a stag, a goose, a wolf and a bear. After his death the people of Farstoke set them upon the four gates, so for evermore they would remember the beautiful animals that had once stood guard, and the boy who had helped them save the town.

So the truth is there are good Farstokers, and there are bad Farstokers. But as far as a lifeling is concerned there's not a speck of difference between the two. William loved Peony, but he still took her life.

They just can't help themselves.

CHAPTER 29

"This is my wife, Alison." Mr Voss opens the bedroom door. "But you've met her already, I think?"

Everything about Alison is even smaller today.

She's a smaller hump in the bed. A smaller rise and fall of the covers.

"You were part of this trip out yesterday, I understand," says Mr Voss.

"Um, yes, I—"

"It was too much for her." He goes over to the window and pulls it shut. "You do know that, don't you?" He locks it firm and takes out the key.

Too much for her.

Is that why she looks so small now?

Is it my fault?

Like the chickens?

Like Suki?

He draws the curtain. The metal rings scrape across the rail. "Bit cold up here, isn't it?"

No. Not really.

"What did you want to show me, Mr Voss?"

"I, um, just wanted you to meet Alison again. She's not well, you see." He sits down on the edge of her bed. Strokes her hair.

She moves, ever so slightly, under the covers.

He bends down. Kisses her head. When he sits back up there are tears in his eyes.

He takes the largest photograph from the bedside table. "They don't know what's wrong with her," he says.

I nod.

"So they don't know how to fix her." He hugs the photograph to his chest. Just like Dad hugging Mum's album. "But maybe you can make it all right now, Lonny. Maybe can you save her."

Me?

"I don't know what we'll do without her – the girls and me." He kisses the top edge of the photo frame, puts it back on the bedside table. It's a picture of all four of them: Mr Voss, Erin, Katy – and Alison. "But you can save her, Lonny." He stands up, looks me straight in the eye. "Tell me the truth. You didn't really come for Suki, did you? You came for Alison.

You answered our prayers. You appeared, when we needed you most."

"No, Mr Voss, that's not... I mean... I can't help Alison. I don't have the buzzing."

"The buzzing?"

"Yeah. I don't have it."

"What's the buzzing?"

"It's a feeling you get, when you're a lifeling. You can only save something, or some*one*, if they're just about to die. That's what makes me get the buzzing. Then I can save them."

"I see. Yes. I remember now. From the stories. But she's terribly ill. Can't we bring the buzzing on somehow? Speed it up?"

"No! And Alison's not... I mean, she's not..." I look at the hump in the bed. Erin's mum. Jess's daughter. "I mean, she's still OK, Mr Voss. Right now she's still OK."

"It's only a matter of time, though," he whispers. "Surely there's something you can do?"

"You can't speed up the buzzing, Mr Voss. You just have to, well, *wait*, I suppose."

"*Wait?*" He flips the bottom of his tie in and out of his fingers. The tiny fox faces bend and curl. *Bushy-bottomed blighters.*

"Yes."

Wait.

And what if I did?

What if I waited here and got the buzzing and saved

Alison?

How old is she? I peer round Mr Voss to look at the photograph. About the same age as Dad? He's thirty-four. If she's thirty-four, she could maybe live another sixty or seventy years.

So if I *did* wait, and I *did* get the buzzing, and I *did* save her, I'd end up an old man. An old, wrinkled man. Just like in the stories.

"And then?" says Mr Voss. "When the buzzing comes? What happens then?"

"Um, well, it'd be really strong. She's not a dog or a rabbit or a chicken. She's a person."

"Yes. She most definitely is."

I lean round to look at the photograph again. The Alison in the picture looks so different – so completely different from the sick person in the bed. Her skin's not yellow, her cheeks aren't hollow, her hair's not flat. And she looks, well, *familiar*. Mr Voss moves aside. I step in, look closer.

"The buzzing'd be almost impossible to resist." I'm talking to Mr Voss but I keep my eyes on the photo. Have I seen her somewhere before? This brighter, fuller Alison?

On TV?

Or perhaps it's just her likeness to Erin and Katy.

"Well, in that case…" Mr Voss is at the door. "In that case I'm afraid I'm going to have to leave you here, Lonny. I'm sure you'll understand. I'm going to, um, well—"

He stops talking and slips quickly out on to the landing.

"Mr Voss?"

He shuts the door behind him.

"Mr Voss, what are you—"

Clunk. He turns the key in the lock.

"Mr Voss!"

"I'm sure you understand, Lonny," he calls through the closed door. "I mean, of course you understand. Just like Jess said, this was all meant to happen. It's your, um, *destiny.*"

My destiny?

I twist the handle. It's not budging.

"Mr Voss, I don't think that's true. I mean, maybe I was meant to save Suki, I don't know." I rattle the handle. "What I mean is, we just came to Farstoke to earn some money. To buy some food. Mr Voss? Mr Voss? Are you still there, Mr Voss? Mr Voss?"

I bend down and look through the keyhole. I can see right into the hall.

He's taken the key.

I turn round. Lean back on the door.

The more good and dandy it seems, Lonny, the more worse it is.

I slide all the way down till I'm small and crouched. Shoulders hunched, like Dad in front of his bonfire.

There are good Farstokers, and there are bad Farstokers. But as far as a lifeling is concerned there's not a speck of difference between the two.

I swallow.

They just can't help themselves.

How have you managed this, Lonny? How have you got yourself into this mess?

I can hear Alison's breath. Short, tight, uneven. And faint festival noise, through the locked window.

I thought it was so clean and tidy in here when I came in yesterday, but it's not really. Not when you look at it from this angle. There are smudges on the skirting boards, balls of dust in the corners, piles of things under Alison's bed.

The Vosses aren't so perfect after all, then.

There are clothes under the bed. Clothes and papers and boxes. Alison's stuff, I s'pose. It'll all still be there, when she's gone. And Erin and Katy'll be just like me. No mother, just a pile of musty old useless belongings instead.

But hold on – what's that?

Something raspberry-coloured. With little white hoops all over it.

I slide forward on the smooth wooden floor and crawl under the bed. I pull the something out.

It's a scarf. The scarf from my mother's photo album.

Alison's breath stumbles. She shifts under her covers. "Philip?" Her voice is hardly even a whisper now. It's a barely-there croak. "Philip?"

I stand up. "It's not Philip, Mrs Vo– I mean, Alison.

It's me, Lonny. Lonny from yesterday." I hold up the scarf. "Alison, can you tell me... Where did you get this?"

"Lonny? What...? Why...?" Her voice trails off.

"Where did you get this scarf?"

Mr Voss is right. She's way worse today. Her face is gaunter, yellower. She doesn't even try to lift her head from the pillow. But the edges of her mouth twitch into a smile.

"A friend gave it to me," she says. "What are you doing here, Lonny?"

"What friend? What was her name?"

She reaches a weak hand out from under the covers and touches the hooped material. "Maria. My lovely friend, Maria."

Maria.

I scrunch the scarf to my face. I breathe her in.

My tears soak into the deep, pink cloth.

CHAPTER 30

Alison lips are cracked and dry. Her head's heavy on the pillow. "Do you know Maria?" she says. Her voice is getting even more raspy.

I nod. "Yes. Maria Kemp. She was my mother."

"Your mother?" Alison croaks. "Is she—"

"She's dead," I say.

"Dead? Oh no. Oh no. I'm so sorry."

"Were you really friends?"

"Yes. Good friends. But –" Alison licks her dry lips – "it was years ago now."

"Would you like some of your water?"

I pick up the glass from her bedside table. She pushes herself up a little from the pillow and sips.

"Can you tell me about her?" I put the water back down and sit on the edge of the bed. I spread my mother's scarf over my lap. "I can't remember much, see? And my dad won't tell me anything."

Alison tries to reach for something under the bed.

"Do you need any help?" I say.

She collapses back on the pillow. "There's a box. It's got flowers on it."

I duck under the bed again. Push some clothes to one side. Here – a cardboard box covered in floral paper, peeling off at the corners. I pull it out.

"Open it up," she says.

I lift the lid. It's jammed full of papers and photographs and little bits of wrapping and all kinds of labels and receipts and tickets.

"Memories," says Alison.

I pick out a card. Open it up. Read it out.

"*Congratulations on your engagement, best wishes, Ron and Dibs.*"

Alison smiles. "Keep looking through," she says, eyes fixed on the box.

I sort through letters and cards and pictures.

I find a small white plastic tag with *Baby Voss* and a date written on in blue pen.

"Erin's hospital tag," says Alison. "From when she was born."

I even find a lock of soft, feathery hair.

Alison almost manages a laugh. "Katy's, I think."

And then – four photographs.

Northgate, Eastgate, Westgate, Southgate.

Stag, wolf, bear, goose.

It's a bright sunny day. In the first three Alison's standing underneath the gates on her own. But in the fourth she has a friend with her.

A friend in a green T-shirt with white letters on it.

A friend in a raspberry-coloured scarf.

Of course.

Alison is Mum's friend from the Southgate photograph.

Of course she is.

"We met at university," whispers Alison. "She came and stayed with us afterwards."

"In Farstoke?"

Alison gives a weak nod. "We had so much fun. Maria was such a free spirit. I shouldn't have been surprised when she left. That's just what she was like, in a way. But I missed her. I missed her terribly."

A free spirit.

That's just what she was like.

All the things I've forgotten. All the things I never knew in the first place. All the things Dad and Grandad won't tell me. Alison knows it all.

"What else was she like?" I say. "How did you meet? Did you know her after I was born? Did you see her with me? Did she... I mean, did she ... did she...?"

It's the biggest question of the lot and I can't even say it.

"Did she love you?" Alison's voice is weakening.

She reaches out. Touches my cheek.

Burnt edges. Broken wings.

"Of course she did."

My eyes blur with tears. I rub them away. I want to see the photo, clear as I can.

"There's a letter in there too," says Alison. "From Maria. Can you see it?"

I fumble in the box. Pull out the next letter I can find. I slip it out of the envelope and skip to the bottom.

All my love,

Maria K.

Short, round handwriting. All the letters wanting to be "o"s.

Alison holds out her hand. I pass it to her and she reads it through. Every so often her lips move gently to the shape of a word.

"Poor Maria." Alison's hands drop to her chest, still clasping the letter. "How did she die, Lonny? Was she sick, like me?"

"She died when Midge was born. Never came home from the hospital."

"I'm so sorry. Poor Midge. Poor you." She brings the letter to her lips.

Kisses.

Kind words.

"She met a boy," says Alison, "at the festival. Fell in love. Eddie, I think his name was. The watchmaker's son."

"My dad."

She smiles. "Yes. One moment she was here, living with us, and the next she was gone. Just like that. Without even saying goodbye. And then I got this letter." She holds it out to me. "You should have it, Lonny. You and Midge. And the scarf, too. I don't need them any more. I'll be gone soon. You should keep them. Here, you read it."

Dear Alison,

By the time you find this I won't be in the house any more, or even in the town, so please don't wear yourself out searching for me. I'm so sorry. I didn't know how to say goodbye, so I've chickened out and run away in the night and left this note instead. Please forgive me. I can't explain exactly why I'm leaving – but, please, you have to believe me when I say I would tell you if I could, I really would, but lives depend upon me not telling anyone. Not just my life, or Eddie's – but the most precious life of all – a brand-new one that hasn't even been born yet. Yes, I'm pregnant – I can tell you that much – but please keep it a secret – please.

Don't worry about me. I am well – really well – and I'm excited about my new future. Even as I write I have my other hand on my belly – I can't believe there's a whole new person in there growing all the time. You mustn't try to find me – promise you won't. I have to stay hidden to keep us all safe.

Did you find the scarf in the parcel? I know you love

it so I want you to have it — and every time you wear it will you think of me?

Thank you for all the wonderful times, Alison. I will come and find you again one day, I promise.

All my love,

Maria K. xxxxxxxxx

"See?" says Alison. "See how much she loved you?"

The most precious life of all.

Me. Lonny Quicke. Chicken-sorting, boot-stuffing Lonny Quicke.

Head's got a little bit calmer.

Heart's grown a little bit stronger.

"She never did come and find me," says Alison. "And I never did find out why she felt she had to disappear. But I didn't tell anyone her secret. Not a soul."

"I know why she disappeared." I take Alison's hands in mine. Letter-saving, secret-keeping hands. "We're a lifeling family."

Alison frowns.

"The Quickes. We're a lifeling family. They would've told her, I s'pose, when she was pregnant. They would've told her the baby could be a lifeling, and that she had to stay in the forest. That's what they do, see? They keep us hidden away. To keep us safe."

"There's no such thing as a lifeling, Lonny. It's just a—"

"No, you're wrong. I'm a lifeling. That's why I'm

here. Why do you think Mr Voss locked me in here with you? He wants me to save you."

"Locked you in? But that's not true, Lonny. Philip wouldn't lock anyone in anywhere."

"Look." I scoot over to the door. Rattle the handle. "I can't open it. And the window, he locked that too." I lope over and try to pull it up. "It's shut fast. He's taken both keys."

"But—"

"Lonny? Lonny?" It's Erin in the hallway, outside the door.

"Erin?" I run over.

"Are you in there, Lonny? What's going on? What has Dad done?"

"Erin." It's Mr Voss. "Come away from there. I told you to stay in the kitchen."

"Lonny?" says Erin. "Are you all right? Is Mum all right?"

"Yes," I call out. "We're—"

"Get away from that door!"

Alison's eyebrows crinkle up. "Philip?" she says, but her voice is so quiet now that no one's going to hear her.

"I'm not going anywhere until you let Lonny out," says Erin.

"Keep out of this, Erin," says Mr Voss. "It's nothing to do with you."

"It's everything to do with me. That's my mum in there, and my friend."

"Your mother's sick."

"I know that."

"She's really sick. Really, *really* sick."

"I know!" shouts Erin.

"Then can't you see what I'm doing? The lifeling boy – he can save her!"

"Philip?" whispers Alison.

"He's not just a *lifeling boy* – he's Lonny. He's my friend."

"And *she's your mother.* And she's *dying.*"

Alison swallows. Blinks back tears.

"Well, if she's dying, why on earth aren't you calling an *ambulance*? Isn't that what we do in the twenty-first century? Give me the key! Lonny? Lonny?" Erin's voice has got louder – she's speaking right through the keyhole. "I'm going to get you out, all right?"

"Get away from that door, Erin."

"Ow. You're hurting me, Dad. You're hurting me!"

Silence.

"What's happening, Lonny?" says Alison. "What's going on?"

I listen.

"I'm ... I'm sorry." Mr Voss. Quieter now. "I don't know what came over me. I'm sorry, Erin, I shouldn't have—"

"Open the door," says Erin. "You have to let him out."

"Yes," says Mr Voss. "Yes. I know. Yes."

The scrape of someone missing the keyhole several times. Then *clunk*, and the door opens.

CHAPTER 31

Erin bursts in past her dad. "Lonny? Mum? Are you OK?"

"We're all right." Alison's voice has nearly disappeared completely. "We're both all right."

Erin rushes over to the bed.

Mr Voss twists his tie. "I, um, I—"

"Phil? Erin?" It's Jess in the hallway. "What on earth is going on?"

"Dad shut Lonny and Mum in here, Gran," says Erin. "He locked them in."

"He did what?"

Mr Voss stands in the middle of the room, blinking. Key in one hand, the end of his tie in the other.

"Right. Let's put that back where it belongs, shall we?" Jess takes the key from him and puts it back in the keyhole on the inside of the door.

"There's the, um, one for the window, too." Mr Voss brings the other key out of his pocket.

Jess takes it over to the window and opens it up. The sounds of the festival leap into the room. The recorder players have returned to Sinkly Square again.

"A frog he would a-wooing go,
Heigh-ho, said Rowley,
A frog he would a-wooing go,
Whether his mother would let him or no.
With a roly-poly, gammon and spinach,
Heigh-ho, said Anthony Rowley."

"I'm, er, I'm sorry, Lonny," says Mr Voss. "I don't know what came over me. I—"

"I'm calling an ambulance," says Erin. "Look at her. I can't believe you haven't called one already, Dad."

"Your mother said I shouldn't," says Mr Voss. "Because of the festival."

"I don't want to spoil it for everyone," croaks Alison.

"She can hardly speak," shouts Erin. "You should've just done it anyway!" She kisses Alison's head. "It's not going to spoil anything, Mum."

"But the gates—"

"It doesn't matter about the stupid gates," says Erin. "They can open them up." She goes to the doorway. "Katy? Katy! Bring the phone up. The landline. Bring it up now!" She turns to me. "You sure you're all right, Lonny?"

I look at the scarf in my hand. The letter. The photograph. "I'm fine," I say. "Really, really fine."

Erin nods. *I'm sorry*, she mouths. "Argh – Suki!" The little dog scampers in and threads herself round Erin's ankles, then Katy and Midge tumble into the bedroom after her.

Katy shoves the phone into Erin's hand. "It's Mum, isn't it?"

Erin stabs at the phone buttons. "Hello?" She holds it to one ear and covers her other while she speaks. "Ambulance. I need an ambulance. It's my mother." She slips out of the bedroom.

"Lonny," says Jess. "Are you really all right?"

"I'm fine."

"I'm so sorry," she says. "Truth is, I never actually thought a lifeling would be, well, a real person, too. Someone we'd all start caring about."

Suki nuzzles my feet.

"I thought our luck was in when you told me you wanted to come to Farstoke," says Jess, "especially when you agreed to bring Midge along too. I thought it was meant to be, and that Alison would be saved and ... well, I got it all wrong, didn't I? Horribly, horribly wrong. Are you sure you're all right? I could never forgive myself if anything happened to you."

I smile. Because I really am fine. I'm probably the finest I've ever been in my whole life. "Look." I hold up the photograph. "Alison knew my mother."

"Is that her?" says Midge. "Can I see?"

"They're coming." Erin hurries back into the room. "Quick, Dad – you've got to go and get them to open the Eastgate."

"She's right, Phil," says Jess. "I can't believe I'm saying it, but we need to get the gate opened."

Mr Voss runs his fingers through his hair. "Yes. Yes. OK."

"Now," says Erin. "Quick!"

"Right. Yes. Thank you, Erin. Thank you." He rushes out of the room and his feet thunder down the spiral stairs.

"Well, I'll be blowed." Jess finishes reading the letter. "You kept that secret a long time, Alison."

But Alison doesn't move. There's just a slow, uneven lift and lower of the covers as she breathes. Suki's curled up on the end of the bed.

"Oh," says Jess. "She's fallen asleep."

"Do you remember her?" I ask. "My mother?"

"*Our* mother," says Midge.

"Absolutely I remember her." Jess passes the letter back to me. "I had no idea she was your mother, though."

"Can I read it?" says Midge.

I tuck it into my pocket.

"In fact," says Jess, "she's popped into my mind on more than one occasion recently, especially since Ken died. She had a very interesting outlook on life."

"Interesting? What do you mean? What was she like?" The questions all flood back into my mind.

"She was a very unique young lady. I'm so sorry you lost her, boys. I really am so sorry."

Unique.

A free spirit.

I want to know everything – *everything* – anyone can tell me. "What else do you remember? I mean, what did she wear? What did she sound like? Did she—"

"I didn't know her as well as Alison did, of course," says Jess. "She only spent a short time with us – a few months, I think, when we lived on Bridge Street. But she was tall, just like you. And just rather ... *unusual.*"

"Unusual? What do you mean?"

Jess smiled. "She was wise, I think now. Infuriated me at the time, though."

"Why? What happened? What did she do?"

"She never wore a watch. Didn't hold with mobile phones, either. Meant she never knew what the time was, so she was always late for absolutely everything. Drove me bonkers. I asked her about it once."

"What did she say?"

"It's strange – I remember it so well. She said she didn't care too much for time. Said she didn't want to know how much time had gone by and how much time there was left because – hold on, let me get this right – *because it's what you do in the right now that really matters."*

I repeat the words under my breath.

It's what you do in the right now that really matters.

I want to remember everything. *Everything.*

"Back then I thought she was quite dotty," said Jess. "And she wasn't completely right, was she? I mean, of course time's important. It's how the whole world runs. You can't go around being late for everything all over the place. But she wasn't completely wrong, either. Sometimes you really do have to put time to one side and make the *right now* the thing that really matters. I think that more and more since Ken died. I like to think Ken believed it too. I think that's what he had in mind when he went out and bought Celia."

"But what else?" I say. "What other things did she do?"

Jess shrugs. "That really stuck with me but I can't remember much else, I'm afraid. I was so busy back in those days. It's Alison you really need to speak to. She lived with her for three years, all through university."

Alison. Grey and yellow and thin. Drowning in troubled sleep.

"Is Mum all right?" says Katy. "Gran? Erin? Is she all right?"

Jess and Erin glance at each other.

Vmmmmmmmmm

"It's OK." Jess wraps her arms round Katy. "I'm sure your dad'll get those gates opened soon so the ambulance can get here quick."

Vmmmmmmmmmmmmm

I press my fingers against my lips.

It's nothing. Really. It's nothing. It's just an itch or something.

Vmmmmmmmmmmmmmm

An itch. That's all.

"David and Daniel are opening the gate." It's Mr Voss, coming up the stairs. "Everything's going to be all right." He stops in the doorway when he sees us. "What's wrong?"

"They're going to be too late." Katy bursts into tears and runs over to her dad.

Mr Voss lifts her up. The circles under his eyes look bigger and darker than ever. Katy clings on to him, with her legs as well as her arms.

Vvvvvmmmmmmmmmmmmmmmm

Alison is small and hollow on the bed.

I squeeze the sides of my jaw.

"OK," says Mr Voss, "everyone needs to go downstairs. There are too many people in here. Everyone out of the bedroom – right now."

"But the ambulance'll be here soon," says Erin. "So it'll all be fine, won't it? They'll get her to the hospital in no time."

The hospital?

"Out of the bedroom, come on." Mr Voss carries Katy to the doorway and sets her on her feet.

"They're taking her to the *hospital*?" I say.

"Yes," says Erin. "So she'll be fine."

"But…" People don't always come home from the hospital. They get taken in, but they don't come home.

Alison rasps quiet open-mouthed breaths.

Vvvvvmmmmmmmmmmmmmmmmmmm

"Why can't they treat her here?" I let Mr Voss herd me towards the door with the others. "Why can't they make her better here, in your house?"

"Listen, right now she needs peace and quiet," he says. "So everyone out, please."

Jess steers Katy, Midge and Suki towards the stairs.

"But, Dad," says Erin, "I think I should stay here with her. I think she needs—"

"Erin, please. I'll give you a shout if there's any change. We need you down there anyway, to let the ambulance crew in – go on."

Erin steps backwards out of the doorway.

"Thank you," says Mr Voss. "Now, you too, Lon—"

I shove him on to the landing.

"Lonny! What are yo—"

I slam the door shut and turn the key.

CHAPTER 32

Just me and Alison now.

Me and Alison and all her memories of my mother.

Vvvvvvvvvvvvvvvvmmmmmmmmmmmmmmmm

And the buzzing. The swelling, building buzzing. Thickening at the back of my throat.

"Lonny!" Mr Voss bangs on the door. "That's my wife in there. Let me in."

I walk over to the bed. The recorders are still playing outside.

*"My grandfather's clock was too tall for the shelf
So it stood ninety years on the floor."*

Vvvvvvvvvvvvvvvvvvvvvvvvmmmmmmmmmm

Alison's breath rattles.

The healthy, rosy Alison beams out from the photograph on her bedside table. Erin and Katy and Mr Voss beam too.

"Lonny?" Mr Voss calms his voice. "Listen to me. Alison is very ill. I shouldn't have locked you in earlier. It was wrong, OK? But I've called an ambulance now, so we need you to open the door."

Vvvvvvvvvvvvvvvvvvvvvvvvvmmmmmmmmmmm

The back of my head.

The deep of my ears.

The pits of my eyes.

"They'll be here any minute," says Mr Voss, "and we need to let them in, OK? We need to let the ambulance crew in, so they can help Alison."

To take her to the hospital?

No. She'll go to the hospital and that'll be the last time we ever see her.

Erin and Katy won't have a mum any more.

Jess won't have a daughter.

Mr Voss won't have a wife.

And the very last memories of my mother will slip through my fingers all over again.

VVVVVVVVVVVVVVVVVVVVVMMMMMM

The buzzing pulls me towards the bed.

I kneel down, my face level with hers.

VVVVVVVVVVVVVVVVVVVVVVVMMMM

My teeth vibrate.

"Lonny? It's Jess. Can you hear me? You need to open the door, love. I got it all wrong. It's not your destiny. Just unlock the door. We won't tell anyone about your secret. We promise. Just let us in, love."

I put a hand on the crisp white covers. A door-locking, life-saving hand.

"Midge is downstairs," says Jess. "He's so upset, Lonny – come down and see him. He's so worried about you."

VVVVVVVVVVVVVVVVVVVMMMMMMMM

Tongue.

Lips.

Cheeks.

Ears.

Eeeeeeee-awwwwwwww – eeeeeeeee-awwwwww – eeeeeeeawwwwwww.

"Hear that? That's the ambulance, Lonny," says Mr Voss. "They're here."

NEEEEEEE-AWWWWWW – NEEEEEEEE-AWWWWW – NEEEEEEE-AWWWWWW.

"Ninety years without slumbering; tick, tock, tick, tock.

His life's seconds numbering; tick, tock, tick, tock."

VVVVVVVVVVVVVVVVVMMMMMMMMM

"Lonny?" Another voice from the hallway.

I blink. It's Erin.

"Lonny?" she says. "Listen, the ambulance has just pulled up outside. Can you hear me?"

A flicker of movement under Alison's shadowed eyelids.

A twitch in her face.

"Lonny?" says Erin. "You can hear me. I know you can. So speak to me. Speak to me!"

I hold my buzzing jaw.

"Can. You. Hear. Me?"

VVVVVVVVVVVVVVVVVVVMMMMMM

I close my buzzing eyes. "Yes."

"Pardon?"

"Yes. I can hear you. Go away."

"Let us through." A fourth voice. "In there, is she? Out of the way, please." A hard knock on the door. "Excuse me, this is Meena Kumari and Claire Matthews – ambulance crew. You need to let us in. We understand there's a lady in need of our immediate attention." *Knock knock knock.* "You really do need to open the door right now, sir, or we'll be forced to call the police."

VVVVVVVVVVVVVVVVVVVMMMMMM

I press my hands against my ears.

"No – not yet," says Erin. "Let me talk to him. Can you hear me, Lonny?"

Breathe, Lonny. Breathe.

"I can hear you," I tell her.

"Will you come to the door? So I don't have to shout?"

I take hold of the bed frame.

VVVVVVVVVVVVVVVVVVVMMMMMM

I push myself up.

I haul myself away from the buzzing and step towards the door.

221

Left foot.

Right foot.

Left foot.

Right foot.

If I keep putting one foot in front of the other, I'll get there.

Left foot.

Right foot.

Left foot.

Right foot.

Hand on the door.

Chicken-sorting. Boot-stuffing.

VVVVVVVVVVVVVVVVMMMMMMM

The buzzing drags at me.

"I'm here," I say.

"Good," says Erin. "That's good. Now, you have to let the ambulance crew in. You have to let them take her to hospital."

"My mum went to hospital."

Silence.

"She never came home," I say.

"I know," says Erin. "And I'm sorry. I'm terribly, terribly sorry. But that's not what always happens. It isn't even what mostly happens. Mostly people come home. They get better, and they come home."

"They don't know how to make your mum better."

Silence.

"But this time might be different," she says. "We have to give them a chance. That's how we do things now. With medicine. We need to do it our way, Lonny."

"But I can save her. I can save her for sure."

"Who *is* this?" says one of the ambulance crew. "What's he talking about? Thought you said he was a kid. Look, if he doesn't let us in we'll—"

"Hold on!" says Erin. "Just give me a bit longer. Lonny? Lonny? What about the things you told me about? Your map. All the places you want to visit. What about London? And Versailles? And Prague?"

The tower.

The palace.

The lane.

"You still want to see them, don't you?" says Erin. "All those places your mother went to?"

Yes. I still want to see them. I still want to go.

VVVVVVVVVVVVVVVVVMMMMMMM

"So you have to open the door," she says. "You have to let these people in."

"But Alison might die."

"Yes." Erin's voice goes quieter. "She might."

I step closer in. My mouth almost touching the door. "Don't you want her saved?"

"What's he talking about?" The ambulance crew mumble in the background.

"Of course I want her saved," says Erin. "But you're my friend. I want you saved, too."

I rest my throbbing, buzzing head on the wood.

VVVVVVVVVVVVVVVVVMMMMMMM

Walk away, Lonny.
Walk away.
I reach down.
I turn the key.

CHAPTER 33

The ambulance crew burst in. "Mrs Voss? Mrs Voss? I'm Meena, and this is Claire. We're from the ambulance service."

VVVVVVVVVVVVVVVVVMMMMMMMM

Erin and Jess and Mr Voss stare at me.

VVVVVVVVVVVVVVVVVMMMMMMMM

I press my hands to my jaw. Squeeze my eyes tight shut.

VVVVVVVVVVVVVVVVVMMMMMMMM

"Lonny? What's wrong?" says Erin. "What's—"

"Nothing."

VVVVVVVVVVVVVVVVVMMMMMMMM

"Nothing!" I squeeze my head. Try and block out

the buzzing.

It doesn't work.

Course it doesn't.

VVVVVVVVVVVVVVVMMMMMMMM

Meena and Claire are pulse-taking and soft-talking and chest-listening.

VVVVVVVVVVVVVVVVMMMMMMMM

"Lonny," says Erin, "how can I help you? What do I need to do?"

VVVVVVVVVVVVVVVVMMMMMMMM

Walk away, Lonny.

No. *Run. Run* away.

I push past Erin.

I leap to the stairs, grab the banister, swing myself round and down, round and down, round and down.

VVVVVVVVVVVVVVVVMMMMMMMM

I run through the perfect clean hall, out through the perfect clean door into fresh air.

Sinkly Square.

Green canopy.

Festival sunshine.

Crowds of Farstokers.

"Three! Three! The rivals!

Two! Two! The lily-white boys!"

And – *whack* – I run straight into something. Some*one*.

His hands grip my arms.

Watchmaking, bonfire-building, album-burning hands.

VVVVVVVVVVVVVVVMMMMMMMM
"Dad?"

He's wet and shivery, cold and pale. A line of blood trickles down his forehead to the inside of his left eye.

"Lonny." His voice croaks like Alison's. He pulls me into him, shoves his face into my baggy green jumper and sobs.

VVVVVVVVVVVVVVVMMMMMMMM

He squeezes me tighter. Thumbs pressing into my ribs. Nose pressing into my shoulder. Muscles and knuckles and knots.

"I thought I'd lost you, Lonny. I thought I'd lost you. Couldn't get into the town. The gates were closed. I tried them all. Tried swimming under. Tried everything. I was locked out until they opened up for that ambulance. What's going on? Are you all right?"

"Dad! Lonny!" Midge runs out, Jess chasing after him. Dad starts sobbing all over again.

"Mr Quicke?" Mr Voss comes out too. "Are you Mr Quicke? Are you Lonny's dad?"

"Who are you?" Dad smears his crying away with the back of his hand. "Who the hell are you?"

"Dad," I say, "it's OK, this is Mr Vo—"

"Listen." Mr Voss grasps Dad's wrist. "You have to take Lonny away. You have to take him away from this town right now."

Dad pulls his arm free. "What gives you the—"

"He's right, Mr Quicke," says Jess. "Take Lonny away from Farstoke. He's not safe here. He's not even safe from us, for heaven's sake."

Mr Voss wipes his forehead. "I'm so sorry, Lonny, I'm so—"

"What did you do?" Dad grabs Mr Voss's shirt and tie. Tiny orange foxes, bent and crushed. "What did you do to my son?"

"Dad! Don't!"

"Mr Quicke!" says Jess.

Dad twists Mr Voss's shirt. "WHAT DID YOU DO?"

"Dad!"

"Steady along the path now." Meena and Claire wheel Alison out of the front door. "Steady through the gate."

VVVVVVVVVVVVVVVMMMMMMMM

"I have to go," says Mr Voss. "Please, Mr Quicke, I have to go, it's my wife, they're taking her to hospital."

Dad stares at the small blanketed bump of a person lying on the trolley. He lets go of Mr Voss.

VVVVVVVVVVVVVVVMMMMMMMM

I press my fingers into the sides of my jaw. Open and close my mouth.

"That's your wife?" says Dad.

Mr Voss straightens his tie. "She's very sick."

Dad blinks. "Will she be all right?"

"I don't know."

Meena and Claire slide Alison into the ambulance.

"You'd better go with her," says Dad. Then he grabs Midge and pulls him close to his chest. Midge's cap falls off.

Mr Voss bends down and picks it up. He passes it to Dad. "Mr Quicke," he says, "you have two lovely boys, but please, please keep Lonny away from Farstoke. It's not a good place for him."

"I know that," says Dad.

Part 3:
FOREST

CHAPTER 34

DING-DONG!

BANG! BANG! BANG!

"DOORBELL'S RINGLING!" shouts Grandad. "DOORBELL!"

Well, I'm not getting it. I'm staying right here in my room.

Exactly where I've been all day. Exactly where I've been all day *every* day for almost a week now.

DING-DONG!

BANG! BANG! BANG!

The wall is bare behind me. It's been days since the festival but the map's still folded up in my bag.

No point putting it back up now.

I'm not going anywhere. I won't be going anywhere ever again.

It's not *safe* for me, is it? That's something everyone agrees on. Grandad and Dad and his new best friends Jess and Phil.

No one asked my opinion.

DING-DONG!

BANG! BANG! BANG!

"DOOR!"

I look out of the window. It's Jess. Again. For the millionth time this week.

"Dad, it's Jess!" Blinkin' Midge. Not so quiet any more, is he?

"Jess! Come in, come in." Dad's brand new *my-friends-are-always-welcome-here* voice carries through the house. "Lonny? Yes, I'll call him down. Lon? Lonny? Come down! Jess says she's got good news she wants us all to hear."

I take a breath in, and sigh it back out.

I get up. Still got yesterday's clothes on.

I sit on a step halfway down the stairs. I can hear whatever she has to say from here.

"Hello, Lonny." Jess beams up at me.

"Aren't you coming all the way down, Lon?" says Dad. Like he hasn't spent twelve full years telling me to go *up* the stairs every time anyone comes to the door.

"No," I say.

"You stay wherever you're comfortable, Lonny,"

says Jess. "Firstly – the best news of all. Remember we told you about the doctor who's on a posting from Spain? The one who thought Alison had a condition that none of the doctors here had ever come across? Can't remember what it was called now – something beginning with S, I think. Well, she was right. She's been treating Alison – and she's getting better. She's on the mend. She's going to be OK!"

A wide smile spreads across Dad's face. "That really is the best news I've heard in a very long time." He opens his arms wide and gives Jess a huge hug. "That's wonderful news, isn't it, boys?"

We nod. Because it is.

Erin and Katy'll have their mother.

Mr Voss'll have his wife.

Jess'll have her daughter.

And me?

I'll have a few more scraps of memory to occupy myself with while I'm stuck here *staying safe* in the forest.

"Sit down, Jess." Dad pulls a chair out from the table. "I'll make some tea."

"Oh no, not yet, not yet. I've got a surprise – hang on." She flings the front door open wide and no one closes it after her. There are tassels on the back of her jacket. They swish as she crunches across the gravel.

She opens Celia's side door and grabs a – hold on – is that a *cage*?

A cage – with a bird in it?

"It's a cockerel!" says Midge.

A blinkin' cockerel.

"You won't believe what happened, Lonny." Jess edges in through the door with the cage. "I did a house-clearance job for a gentleman whose mother had passed away, and he was looking for a happy home for this little fella! I told him – our stars must have aligned. There was you needing a cockerel, and there was him trying to rehome one! It was meant to be."

Meant to be?

No, it wasn't. *I* should've bought that cockerel myself. With money that *I* should've earned. That's what *should've* happened. This wasn't *meant to be* at all.

"Chickens aren't allowed inside the house," I say.

"Lonny!" says Dad. "How about a *thank-you*?"

"Oh, please, he doesn't need to thank me." Jess puts the cage on the table. "His name's Newport – I know, don't ask me why. Obviously you can change that if you want to. I think he looks like a Stanley myself, but it's up to you. Oh, and Eddie, I wanted to ask you something. Do say 'no' if you're too busy – I realise you've probably got plenty of work for Everston's – but if you're interested, I'm looking for someone to finish doing up Celia for me."

"Celia?"

"My caravanette."

"Oh." Dad looks out the window. "I didn't realise

it – or, um, *she* – had a name."

"I've been meaning to finish doing her up myself but I never seem to have the time," says Jess. "So now Phil and Alison are insisting they pay someone to do it for me – for my birthday. Isn't that fantastic? You interested in taking it on, Eddie? Thought it was the sort of thing you might be good at."

"It's a wonderful idea – I'd be delighted to," says Dad. "Brilliant. Let's celebrate with a cup of tea." He snatches up the kettle and shoves it under the tap.

Chuck chuck chuck goes the cockerel.

Jess grins. "Newport obviously likes it here. D'you know, that gentleman didn't want a penny for him? It really was destiny, wasn't it?"

"There's no such thing as destiny." I growl it under my breath.

"Sorry, Lonny? What was that?" Dad frowns at me.

"There's no such thing as blinkin' destiny," I shout. "And what are you even doing here, Jess? Who invited you back? Go away. Go away and leave us alone!"

I run upstairs and drop face down on to my bed.

Why can't everything just go back to normal?

Midge and Dad in the workshop.

Boot-stuffing.

Chicken-sorting.

Mushroom-gathering.

Just like it was before.

CHAPTER 35

Midge opens the bedroom door.

"Go away," I tell him.

"I told Jess you didn't mean it," he says.

"I did mean it."

"You were horrible to her."

"She should leave us alone."

"I like her," says Midge.

"She talks rubbish. All that *this was meant to happen* and *our stars must have aligned* nonsense. That's not how life works. There's no such thing as *destiny*. Things don't happen for a reason. They just *happen*."

Midge stands there saying nothing. For ages. Staring at me.

"She just sees things differently from you," he says eventually. "That's all."

"She's ridiculous."

"No she's not. She's kind. And helpful. And fun."

"And *wrong*."

"She might be wrong or she might be right. I don't know. But she did a good thing. She got us a cockerel. She did a good thing in the *right now*. And that's what matters. Just like Mum said."

Blinkin' Midge.

Blinkin' Jess.

Blinkin' Newport.

Blinkin' forest.

Blinkin', blinkin', blinkin' lifeling.

"I told her you were tired," he says, "and that you didn't mea—"

BANG! BANG! BANG!

Oh great. Not again.

"WHERE'S MY AFTERNOON CUPPA?"

"Shut up, Grandad!" I can't stand it any more. I just can't stand it. "Shut up!"

"Now you're being horrible to Grandad!" says Midge. "All he wants is some company. That's all he ever wants, really. Can't you even see that?"

"S'GONE FOUR! WHERE ARE YOU ALL?"

BANG! BANG! BANG!

Midge goes across the landing and into Grandad's room. "Hi, Grandad," he says. "There's some good news about Alison."

I jump up and slam our bedroom door shut.

I don't want to hear any more about other people's good news.

I draw the curtains to shut out the forest and the sky and the whole wide world. But daylight still seeps through.

I curl up in bed, soaked in pink light.

One is one and all alone
And evermore shall be so.

An hour or so later it's quiet. Grandad's not banging. No sound of Jess nattering or Midge fretting. I go downstairs. Peer into the workshop.

"Lonny? You OK?" Dad flips up his working specs. He puts the watch he's working on into the wooden box. He closes the lid. "I need to talk to you, Lonny. I've been thinking about what's been going on. And I realise I've been in a tunnel. Not a real tunnel. A metaphorical one. A long, dark metaphorical tunnel. Sorry, that sounds like a cliché, doesn't it? Your mother hated clichés."

My mother?

He's started talking about my mother *now*?

He takes his specs off. Folds the arms. Puts them down on the worktable. "What I'm trying to say is, I've not been well, and I want to thank you for keeping things going. For doing those things you did. Earning money and buying food." He's not looking at me. He's sliding his folded specs side to side between his hands. "Anyway, what I'm trying to say is, I think I might be coming out of the tunnel now. I feel like there's a future. Does that make sense? Things are looking up. You don't need to worry any more. You can stay here, safe in the forest. I can earn enough money. I won't be disappearing into my bedroom again for days at a time, or ignoring the fact that no one wants to buy pocket watches any more."

The house is quiet. Silent. Just the *tock tock tock* of the grandfather clock.

He fiddles with the catch on the wooden box. "Do you see what I'm—"

"Where's Midge?" I say.

"Midge? He went back to Farstoke with Jess."

Gone to Farstoke? Without me?

But it was *me* who thought of going there. *Me* who wanted to leave the forest in the first place.

"Why?"

"He wanted to see Katy. And he wanted to go on something before they take it down. Can't remember what it was called now. A *zip* something?"

"The zip wire?"

"That's it. The zip wire. But don't worry, Lon. I spoke to him. He won't tell anyone about you. He really seems to have grown up recently."

But Midge always just wanted to stay at home. In the workshop. Where he fits in.

That's what's right. That's what's normal.

And if he has grown up, that's because of *me*, isn't

it? Because of the things *I* got him to do? Anyone noticed *that*?

"Oh, and guess what," says Dad. "Mr Voss has arranged things so Midge can start school tomorrow. So he'll be going to Farstoke every day."

"*Every day?*"

"Well, Monday to Friday anyway. It'll be great for his future. In fact, it'll be great for all our futures – he'll be able to get a good job and support us when he's older. So you can stay safe in the forest."

A monster stirs inside me. An ugly, angry, forest-dwelling ogre. With clodhopper boots and ham-fisted hands.

"But you teach us just fine, Dad. Here. At home. He doesn't need to go to school."

"But at a proper school he'll get more confident, meet lots of new people. Maybe even get to go out of Farstoke, on some school trips or something. Wouldn't that be great?"

The ogre twists and turns.

It stretches and grows.

It twists and turns and stretches and grows and – *SMACK!*

I punch the worktable with my ogre fist. The wooden box shakes.

"Lonny! What are you—"

SMACK! I punch the table again.

SMACK! SMACK! SMACK!

"Lonny, stop!"

My knuckles bleed angry blood. I suck them clean.

What am I doing?

What am I doing punching the table?

What am I doing even standing here listening to this?

What am I doing in the middle of the forest when everyone else is getting on with their lives?

What am I doing shuffling around this blinkin' house when the whole wide world is sitting there outside and there's a bus in Farstoke that can take you straight to it? *Every two hours, every day of the week.*

What on earth am I *doing*?

CHAPTER 36

Dad drops down on to the bus-stop bench beside me. Puts his head in his hands. Tries to catch his breath. *Huff, puff, huff.*

He followed me all through the forest. Gave up trying to speak to me at the oaks. Gave up trying to grab hold of me. I just shook him off.

He followed me across the dandelion field.

He followed me under the Northgate.

He followed me all the way here to the middle of Farstoke.

"Lonny." He huffs and puffs. Puffs and huffs. Big Bad Wolf. "I'm sorry," he says. "Whatever I've done, I'm sorry."

Whatever I've done?

He doesn't get it, does he?

He still doesn't even get it.

"Lonny, I'm just trying to keep you safe. You've seen what can happen. Even when you're with good people. When they find out who you are and what you can do, they do terrible things. I promised your mother I'd keep you safe."

Don't.

Don't even mention my mother.

Don't even pretend you know what she'd want.

She wouldn't want anyone shut up in the forest for their whole life. She was *a free spirit.*

"And as we're on the subject of your mother –" *huff, puff* – "I know I haven't told you enough about her."

Shut up, shut up, shut up. I don't want to hear. It's too late. I've figured it out for myself. I'm going to London, Edinburgh, Versailles, Prague. I'm going to all the places she went to. I'll stand exactly where she stood and see all the things that she saw.

"It's been too painful, you see, Lon."

The photograph album might be lost in the bonfire but I haven't forgotten the pictures. They're burned into my mind. And I'll write to Alison. She's getting better now. She can tell me everything she remembers. She can write it down in letters and I'll keep them forever.

"But I've been thinking about it –" *huff, puff* – "and

speaking to Jess and Phil about it and I'm going to set it all right..."

Here we go again.

Jess this, Phil that. Blah, blah, blah, blah –

Oh – there – the bus. It's coming.

I stand up. Grab my rucksack.

"Lonny, you can't be serious about this." Dad stands up too. "Where are you going to go? I know you look older but you're still only twelve for goodness' sake."

The bus gets closer and closer. Bigger and bigger.

I pull the rucksack on to my back.

Vmmmmmmm

What was that?

Nothing.

I rub my lips.

It was nothing.

"How on earth will you support yourself? And how do you think you're going to..."

Dad rambles on about pointless stuff and I give up listening because the bus is nearly here.

It stops at the zebra crossing. A very old lady puts her stick into the road, then shuffles forward a couple of centimetres.

She puts her stick a bit further forward and shuffles after it again.

It's going to take her a hundred years to get across. She should be sat at home like Grandad. Not out here holding up other people's buses.

Vvvvvvmmmmmmmm

I press my lips. Another stupid insect most likely.

"– and what you have to remember, Lon," Dad carries on, "is that you've led a very sheltered life and—"

"Help! Help!"

Dad stops. He frowns.

"Help!"

It's coming from the river. Where we went with Alison, that first day in Farstoke.

"Someone's in trouble," says Dad.

Vvvvvvmmmmmmmmmm

The thick of my tongue.

The roots of my teeth.

"Help! *Please!* Someone help!"

"Stay here, Lonny. I'm going to go and see what's going on." He grabs my shoulders. Fingers digging in. Muscles and knots. "Don't get on the bus. Please don't." He lopes away towards the river.

Vvvvvvvvvvvvvvmmmmmmmmmmmmmmmm

I cover my ears. Don't know why. It never makes any difference.

Vvvvvvvvvvvvvvvvvvvvmmmmmmmmmmmm

Stop. Just stop.

No more buzzing.

No more buzzing!

The old lady finally makes it across the road and the bus pulls up in front of me.

Vvvvvvvvvvvvvvvvvvvvvmmmmmmmmmmmm

I need to get away from here.

Three people are getting off. A girl, older than me, and two men. The girl has a suitcase with wheels on it. She stops as soon as she steps off the bus and bends over to mess about with the case, blocking the exit. The men behind grumble at her. She pulls out a handle, then sets off towards the square, *trrrrrrrundling* the case behind her.

Vvvvvvvvvvvvvvvvvvvvvvvvvvvvvvvvvvvvvmmmmm

"Help! Help!"

Dad? Was that Dad?

"You getting on or what?" says the bus driver.

I glance behind me. I'm the only one waiting.

The only one waiting to go to London and Edinburgh and Versailles and Prague. To freedom. To LIFE. To my mother.

"Help!"

Thud-thud-thud-thud-thud. A fist banging on front doors.

A desperate, panicking, door-banging fist.

A desperate, panicking, door-banging, *watchmaking* fist.

"Please, somebody," Dad shouts. "I don't have a phone. We need an ambulance!"

Thud-thud-thud-thud-thud.

Someone opens their door. "Have you got a phone?" yells Dad. "We need someone to call an ambulance. Please, quickly. It's my son. At the river. He needs help. Yes – thank you. Thank you. Thank you."

He skids away from the door, back round the corner

to the river.

My son?

Vvvvvvvvvvvvvvvvvmmmmmmmmmmmmmmmm

The top of my head.

The soft of my cheeks.

Midge?

Vvvvvvvvvvvvvvvvvmmmmmmmmmmmmmmmm

The buzzing pulls at my skin and my bones and my heart and my lungs and my stomach.

Walk away, Lonny.

Get on the bus.

"I can't wait all day, son." The driver taps his watch. "I'm already running late."

Freedom.

LIFE.

My mother.

VVVVVVVVVVVVVVVVVVVVMMMMMMMM

But – Midge.

But – fretty blinkin' Midge.

VVVVVVVVVVVVVVVVVVVVMMMMMMMM

But – fretty, watchmaking, cap-wearing, coin-sorting, friend-making, Grandad-calming, zip wire-flying, motherless, blinkin' Midge.

"You getting on or not?"

I shake my head. "No, thank you," I say. "I've changed my mind."

CHAPTER 37

I run. Across the road, down past the houses where Dad was knocking on doors. Someone steps out, phone clamped to his ear. I dodge him and speed round the corner.

VVVVVVVVVVVVVMMMMMMMMMM

A tiny huddle of people, stooped and crouched on the riverbank. Erin's there. And Dad. And someone else – David from Farstoke Groceries. All kneeling beside a … a *body*.

David, he's kissing it – no – blowing breath into it. Into Midge.

The kiss of life.

David kneels up, interlocks his fingers and presses

his hands into Midge's chest.

Press-press-press-press-press-press-press-press-press-press-press-press.

And everything. Slows. Right. Down.

There's Katy on the other bank. Her hair is sopping wet. Her *clothes* are sopping wet. Daniel is with her. He takes off his jacket and wraps it round her. She coughs and splutters and pulls the coat close under her chin, just like she did with the lifeling cloak.

There's something in the water. Something yellow. Midge's hat.

VVVVVVVVVVVVVMMMMMMMMMM

The buzzing pulls and twists and drags at me.

VVVVVVVVVVVVVMMMMMMMMMM

Lips, teeth, cheeks.

VVVVVVVVVVVVVMMMMMMMMMM

Ears, throat, eyes.

So.

Here I am.

Here I am, in the *right now*, standing behind Dad and Erin.

Just an arm's length away from my dying brother.

He is grey.

And wet.

And limp.

Press-press-press-press-press-press-press-press-press-press-press-press.

His body jerks with every beat of David's hard-working hands.

But he doesn't *move*.

He doesn't *live*.

Lifeless.

LIFE.

LESS.

"How long will the ambulance take?" Dad shouts at David. "How long? HOW LONG?"

David doesn't answer.

David presses.

David blows.

Midge doesn't move.

"Erin?" says Dad. "How long? HOW LONG?"

"I don't know," says Erin. She turns round. Sees me right behind her. "Lonny! It's all right – we've called an ambulance. It'll be all right."

Dad stares at me. "Lonny," he says. "You should go. Walk away."

VVVVVVVMMMMMMMMM

Press-press-press-press-press-press-press-press-press-press-press-press.

"What happened?" My words don't sound like my own. They sound like they belong to someone else. Someone far, far away.

"Katy fell in," says Erin. "They wanted to stop off to play Poohsticks on the way back from the zip wire. She was being silly, messing about on that step thing on the bridge. Midge jumped straight in after her. Didn't even hesitate. I saw it all. He saved her, Lonny.

He pushed her out. He saved her life."

A mayfly flits in front of my face.

I swish it away.

Press-press-press-press-press-press-press-press-press-press-press-press.

David presses.

David blows.

Midge is wet.

Midge is limp.

Midge is blue.

VVVVVMMMMMMMMMM

Tick. Tock. Tick. Tock.

I push myself in between Dad and Erin.

Life's seconds numbering.

"No!" Dad grabs me.

I shove him away.

I kneel down.

I reach out a hand.

A chicken-sorting, boot-stuffing, money-earning, dog-poisoning, life-giving hand.

And I stroke Midge's cheek.

Feels soft. And warm. Like kisses and kind words from your mother.

I haven't had either of those in a very long time.

And Midge has never had them at all.

"Lonny! Don't, Lonny!" Erin. All fretty. Too late.

VVVVMMMMMMMMMM

The buzzing shifts. Shudders down my neck. Squeezes past my shoulder, my elbow, my hand. Pushes out through the ends of my fingers.

Dad pulls my arms. But we're fixed together, me and Midge. Forest brothers. And the buzzing flows like blood, into his bones and his flesh and his breath.

Midge jerks.

Midge gasps.

Midge coughs.

Midge jolts and grabs and sits up and shouts and cries.

Just like magic.

And the buzzing's gone.

I fall on to the ground.

Can't get up.

Too weak.

"What in heaven's name just happened?" David's voice is muffled in my ear.

"Lonny? Lonny?" Erin bends over me. "Can you hear me, Lonny?" She's muffled too. Her hair falls like a curtain in front of my eyes.

The riverbank grass is cold and damp under the side of my face.

Give a bit of life, lose a bit of life.

That's how it goes.

EPILOGUE

It takes *concentration,* walking down the stairs.

I need to grip the banister with my papery, wobbly hand and look carefully at each foot as I move it.

It takes *concentration* and *time*.

Right foot down on to the first step, then join it with the left.

Right foot down on to the second step, then join it with the left.

Right foot down on to the third step, then join it with the left.

You get the picture.

It takes *concentration* and *time* and *pain.*

My knees grind with every step. My hips crunch.

My back pinches.

It takes *concentration* and *time* and *pain* and *energy*.

I'm not surprised Grandad gave up coming downstairs altogether. By the time I reach the bottom I'm exhausted. I grope my way over to the kitchen armchair and collapse into it.

Nothing happens in the middle of the forest. It's impossibly far away from the rest of the world. Especially for an old grey quiver of a man who's not much use for anything at all.

I'll never get to the places from my mother's photograph album.

I'm unlikely even to go back to Farstoke.

But things could be worse, I reckon.

At least we only have fourteen steps, for instance.

At least I don't live in Erin's house with that huge spiral staircase.

"Lonny!" Midge dashes into the kitchen. "They're here, I heard the car!" He flings open the front door and props it steady with one of my old muddy boots.

BANG! BANG! BANG!

"INTERPOLERS!" Grandad starts yelling. "INTERPOLERS!"

"It's *interlopers*, Grandad," Midge calls up. "But they're not anyway. It's Erin and Katy."

Yap! Yap-yap!

Suki. She scampers through the door, spots me here in the chair and leaps on to my lap. She licks my face.

"Blinkin' dog." I stroke the ridiculous trembly

thing, and she settles down. Soft. Warm.

Scrunch-scrunch-scrunch-scrunch. Katy runs across the gravel and into the house. "Suki, you're so naughty! You weren't even invited in."

"Hello, Katy." Dad comes through from the workshop, wiping his hands on a rag. "Good to see you."

Erin stops in the doorway. "D'you want me to put Suki outside?"

"No." I give the silly dog a scratch on the back of her head. Her silky ears flatten down. "She's fine where she is."

"Look!" says Katy. "We brought Mum. She's so much better. Look!" She yanks Erin out of the way and there's Alison being helped from the car by Mr Voss.

She smiles when she sees me. Her skin's not yellow any more. Her cheeks aren't hollow. She's the Alison from the photograph again. Smiling. Squinting in the sunshine.

LIFE.

I give her a weak wave.

HONK! HONK! HONK!

The all-new fixed-up Celia careers into the driveway and screeches to a halt, flinging bits of gravel into the air behind her. Jess steps out in her sparkly boots and an enormous pair of sunglasses. She swings her purple tasselly bag on to her shoulder.

"Jess," says Mr Voss, "you really should be more

careful in that vehicle."

"Please don't fret, Phil. I didn't break any speed limits." She takes Alison's free arm and together they help her into the kitchen.

Alison sinks into a chair. "I know you weren't expecting me but the girls wanted to surprise you. And I wanted to give you these." She fishes around in her bag and brings out Mum's letter, the photograph and the raspberry scarf.

"Mum's things!" says Midge.

Alison lays them carefully on the table.

"Look, Dad, there's the photograph we told you about." Midge picks up the picture. "Maybe we could put it in a frame."

Dad smiles. "I think that's an excellent idea."

Mr Voss sits down next to Alison. "I, um, I…" He darts a little glance in my direction. He's not looked me properly in the eye since festival day. "I thought you might like to know the latest news from Farstoke. Especially, um, especially you, Lonny." Another quick half-look. "We've formed a new festival committee. I'm very proud to say that both Erin and I are now members."

"Yeah," says Erin. "We're going to change the whole thing into something less… Well, less likely to make everyone outside Farstoke think we're crazy."

"What Erin's trying to say," says Mr Voss, "is that we're hoping to move the festival away from being a celebration that promotes rather dangerous ideas about, um, *unusual individuals* –" he shoots me another look – "and make it a festival of life, rather than lifeling. All of us here recognise the immense importance of guarding your family secret – as do David and Daniel, who are already key members of the committee."

"Well, I don't know what to say, Philip. Thank you." Dad props the photograph of Mum and Alison up against a mug in the middle of the table. "That really is fantastic news."

"And we want the gates to be kept open," says Erin, "so anyone can come."

Ting! Ting! Ting!

Jess has found a teaspoon and a glass on the draining board. It's like a bell singing through the house.

"Well, now we've heard the Farstoke news," she says, "I have an announcement of my own."

Alison frowns. "What are you up to, Mum?"

BANG! BANG! BANG!

"WHAT THE GOODNESS GRACIOUS ME IS GOING ON DOWN THERE?"

BANG! BANG! BANG!

"Don't worry, Mr Quicke," Jess calls up the stairs. "This includes you, too." She clears her throat. "I've made a decision. I've decided to go travelling. In Celia. Just like Ken and I planned to before he died. I'm going to follow Maria's philosophy –" she nods at the photograph – "and live as a free spirit in the *right now*. And, Lonny, I'd like to invite you to come with me."

Me?

"What do you say, Lonny?" she says. "We can go wherever we please. It won't exactly be luxury living, but you've never struck me as a luxury-living sort of chap."

"But … I can't."

"Why ever not?"

"Well…" Can't she see? I look down at myself. Frail and crooked in the chair. "I can't. I'm too weak and—"

"Nonsense. You're old, not dead. And I'm inviting your grandfather as well. We need to get him down from that bedroom and back out into the world. There's plenty of room in Celia." She looks up the stairs. "Did you hear that, Mr Quicke? I want you to come travelling with me and Lonny. You up for it?"

"EDDIE! SOMEONE IS ATTEMPTING TO KIDNAPPLE ME! EDDIE? EDDIE? YOU THERE, EDDIE?"

Dad rolls his eyes. "Stop panicking, Dad. It's only Jess."

"Can I come too?" says Katy.

"No you cannot," says Mr Voss. "You have to go to school."

"But why doesn't Lonny have to go to school? He might *look* a hundred but he's only twelve."

"Ka-ty!" says Erin. "He does *not* look a hundred."

"Lonny will be attending the Great School of Life

instead," says Jess. "And please be very careful in whose company you make comments like that, Katy. Remember, we all need to keep the Quicke family secret from now on."

"You should definitely go, Lonny," says Erin. "You can send us postcards. And maybe we can come and visit you in exotic places in the holidays."

"Of course," says Jess.

"Where will you go first, Gran?" says Katy.

"I don't know. Where first, Lonny?"

Where first?

The tower?

The castle?

The palace?

The lane?

How could I even choose?

"When are you planning to leave?" I ask.

"Tomorrow," says Jess. "I'm packed and ready."

"You're what?" says Alison.

"I'm packed and ready. I've even sorted out a rabbit-sitter for Waldo, and Eddie here has agreed to take on my odd-job business."

"Eddie?" says Mr Voss. "Were you in on this?"

Dad smiles. "Jess and I may have had a few chats while I've been working on Celia."

"So," says Jess, "I'm all set to go first thing. Drawn-out goodbyes are best avoided in my experience. What do you say, Lonny?"

"Tomorrow? But—"

"You got somewhere better to be?"

"Well, no ... but ... what about the chickens? What about Layla?"

"We'll look after the chickens," says Midge.

"Yup," says Dad. "And last time I looked Layla seemed quite happy now that she's got Newport for company."

"Well, that's that one sorted," says Jess. "Any more obstacles, Lonny?"

"Um, I, um…"

"No? Good. Now, who's going to help me get Mr Quicke the Elder down those stairs in the morning?"

"BE NICE IF AN OLD GENTLEMAN COULD BE GENEROUSED WITH A SPOONFUL OF DIGNITY." Grandad frowns out of the open passenger door at everyone in the driveway. He's settled in the front seat of Celia, right between me and Jess. He wasn't too keen on how Dad and Mr Voss got him down the stairs.

He elbows me in the arm and lowers his voice for once. "Imagine if Grandma Quicke could goggle me now, Lonny. Going on a road trip! With a grandson eldier than miself and a twinkly-booted fairy-goodmother in long-legged denims. Just imagine!" He rubs his hands together. Papery, wobbly, excited hands.

Jess turns the key and Celia *thruuummmms*. Dad closes the door for us but the window's still open.

Midge edges himself forward and puts his hand on the bottom of the frame. "I'll miss you, Lonny."

I put my hand on top of his. Unbelievably I'm going to miss him, too.

Katy sticks out a grumpy bottom lip. "I still don't see why I can't come."

"Because you just can't, all right?" It's Erin. My good friend Erin, who's got her whole life stretched out in front of her like a crazy, scary, brilliant zip wire. She's holding Suki in her arms and has to keep twisting her head to escape the licking. "Lonny, don't forget to send postcards, will you? I want to know all the places you visit."

"I won't forget," I tell her.

"Keep safe," says Alison.

"Don't forget to eat," says Dad.

"And for goodness' sake drive carefully," says Mr Voss.

"Will you lot please stop worrying?" Jess puts Celia into gear. "We're old enough to look after ourselves, you know."

Wind blows fresh on my face through Celia's open window. The road weaves through the trees – ash and birch and hazel.

Vvvvvvvvvmmm

A tug on my lip. A pull from the forest. I try to squash it with my fingers.

Grandad eyes me sideways. "I coggle that look,

Lonny," he says.

Jess glances sideways too. "You all right, Lonny? Nerves, is it? Cold feet? Don't worry, it'll pass."

Vvvvvvvvmmmmmmmmm

"You're not seeing it proper, Miss Jessica! That's not freezy-toes. That's a lifeling with a buzzing!"

"A buzzing?" Jess leans forward to look at me better. Celia wobbles on the road. "Is that true, Lonny? Good heavens. Is it your grandad? He's not going to drop dead on us, is he? We've only just set off."

"No, I very most surely and very most definitely am not!" says Grandad. "It's something outside! In the forest!"

Vvvvvvvvvvvmmmmmmmmmmmmmmmm

"Grandad's right," I say. "It's outside. A rabbit maybe. Or a badger."

"Right," says Jess. "In that case wind that window up this second, Lonny Quicke. The handle won't fall off this time – your dad fixed it nicely. Now, Country Hits, anyone?" She turns on the radio, presses her foot down and Celia carries us away from the buzzing and out into the rest of the world.

ACKNOWLEDGEMENTS

I'd like to send my enormous thanks to:

My editor, Kirsty Stansfield, and all the team at Nosy Crow.

Brian Geffen, US editor.

My agent, Nancy Miles.

Illustrators Matt Saunders and David Dean.

Designer Nicola Theobald.

The Swaggers, the Whatnots and the BSU MAWYP class of 2016.

Julie, who read the first few pages of this book at Waterloo Station and encouraged me to write the rest.

Sarah Mussi, who awarded a first prize to an embryonic opening of this book at the Hampshire Writers' Society in 2014.

Maddy, Lu and Evie, who gave me advice on dogs and chickens.

My good friend, Margaret.

Simon, Dennis & Victor.

Janice, Alan and Claire.